AND THE STONES CRY OUT

Also by Clara Dupont-Monod in English translation

The Revolt

Clara Dupont-Monod

AND THE STONES CRY OUT

Translated from the French by
Ben Faccini

MACLEHOSE PRESS
QUERCUS · LONDON

First published as *S'adapter* by Éditions Stock, Paris, in 2021

First published in Great Britain in 2024 by

MacLehose Press
An imprint of Quercus Editions Limited
Carmelite House
50 Victoria Embankment
London EC4Y 0DZ

An Hachette UK company

This book is supported by the
Institut français (Royaume-Uni)
as part of the Burgess Programme

A CIP catalogue record for this book is available from the British Library.

ISBN (HB) 978 1 52943 536 8
ISBN (Ebook) 978 1 52942 537 6

This book is a work of fiction. Names, characters, organisations, places
and events are either the product of the author's imagination or are used
fictitiously. Any resemblance to actual persons, living or dead, events or
particular places is entirely coincidental.

10 9 8 7 6 5 4 3 2 1

Designed and typeset in Haarlemmer by Libanus Press, Marlborough
Printed and bound in Great Britain by Clays Ltd, Elcograf S.p.A.

"I tell you that, if these should hold their peace, the stones would immediately cry out."

Luke 19:40

"What does 'normal' mean?
My mother is normal. My brother is normal.
I have no desire to be like them."

The Leaning Girl
Benoît Peeters and François Schuiten

I

The Firstborn

ONCE UPON A TIME, A MALADAPTED BOY WAS BORN into a family. "Maladapted" is an ugly, demeaning word, but it captures the reality of his limp body and empty, wandering eyes. Terms like "damaged" or "incomplete", which imply an object beyond use, fit for the scrap heap, are too strong. "Maladapted" rightly suggests that this boy lived outside any form of functionality – his hands couldn't grasp and his legs couldn't move – but he existed, all the same, on the edge of other people's lives. True, he was not fully part of them, but he was present, like a shadow in the corner of a painting: disconcerting, yet deliberately placed there by the artist.

The family didn't notice a problem at first. In fact, the baby was rather beautiful. Visitors from the surrounding villages came to see the mother. They slammed their car doors and stretched before taking a few tentative steps;

getting to the hamlet required driving on tiny, winding roads, stomachs turned inside out. Some friends came from nearby mountains – though "nearby" didn't mean much where the family lived. To get anywhere you either had to go uphill or downhill. There was no escaping the steep, rolling slopes. Sometimes, in the hamlet's court-yard, you felt as if you were hemmed in by towering waves waiting to break, their green froth sparkling. When the wind picked up and shook the trees, there was even an ocean-like rumbling. The hamlet then resembled an island sheltered from the storms.

The door into the courtyard was thick, rectangular and studded with black nails. A medieval door, the experts said, which had probably been made centuries earlier by the family's ancestors around the time they settled in the Cévennes. The hamlet's two main houses had been built before the porch, bread oven and wood-shed – and the mill on the other side of the river. You could hear the sighs of relief from inside visitors' cars when the narrow road tapered into a small bridge and the terrace of the first house by the river came into view. Behind it stood the second house where the boy had been born. The mother opened the medieval door to greet her friends and family. She offered them chestnut wine in the shade of the courtyard. Everyone spoke quietly so as not to frighten the well-behaved infant snug in his

cot. He smelled of orange blossom, and looked cheerful
and placid. He had round pale cheeks, dark hair and big
black eyes. He was a typical child of the region, an intrinsic part of it. The mountains watched over his cot like
matriarchs, their feet steeped in rivers, their flanks
clothed in a mantle of wind. The boy belonged in that
landscape like any other. Babies up there had black eyes
and the old were thin and wizened. Everything was how
it should have been.

Three months went by before anyone noticed the boy
didn't babble. He remained silent most of the time, apart
from the odd cry. Sometimes a smile appeared, or a
frown, or a sigh after he finished a bottle of milk.
Occasionally, he got startled when a door slammed. That
was it: a few cries and smiles, a frown, the odd sigh or a
twitch. Nothing else. He didn't wriggle. He stayed calm.
He was "inert", his parents thought without admitting
it out loud. The baby showed no interest in faces, in
dangling mobiles or rattles. Above all, his shadowy eyes
didn't settle on anything. They seemed to rove from side
to side, while his pupils reeled and turned, as if following
the dance of an invisible insect, latching on to nothing
in particular. The boy couldn't see the bridge, the two
houses, or the courtyard separated from the road by an
old wall of reddish stones. The wall had been there

since time immemorial, demolished a thousand times by storms and passing convoys, and rebuilt a thousand times, too. The boy couldn't see the mountains with their flayed skin and slopes thick with trees, streaked by torrents. His eyes swept over landscapes and people without lingering.

One day, when the boy was in his rocker chair, the mother knelt down beside him. She was holding an orange and she moved it gently from side to side in front of his face. His big black eyes didn't lock onto the fruit. They were staring elsewhere. Looking at what exactly, it was hard to say. The mother moved the orange back and forth again several times. She had proof the boy couldn't see properly, or at all.

No-one will ever know what feelings swept through her heart at that precise moment. We, the red stones in the courtyard, who are narrating this story, are devoted to children. We carry their stories deep within us, and it is their tale we wish to tell. We see people's lives from our position embedded in the wall. We've always been witnesses. For the most part, children are the forgotten ones in any story. They are herded around like sheep, ignored more than they're protected. But children are the only ones who play with stones. They name us. They cover us with bright stripes. They scribble over us, paint us, decorate us with eyes and mouths, give us grass for hair, and stack us one on top of the other to create dens. They send us ricocheting and make goalposts and train tracks out of us. While adults use us, children distract us. That's why we care for them. It's a matter of gratitude. Adults forget that they're indebted to the children they once were. We owe it to children to tell this tale. Indeed, we were looking in their direction when the father summoned them into the courtyard.

Plastic chairs were dragged into place by a firstborn boy and his younger sister. Both were dark with black eyes, of course. The firstborn, a mere nine years old, sat bolt upright, his chest puffed out. He had the thin, tough legs of a mountain child, covered in scabs and bruises, legs used to climbing and scrambling over slopes bristling with spiky branches of broom. He instinctively put his hand on his sister's shoulder. He often appeared aloof, but this aloofness stemmed from exalted, romantic ideals. He valued endurance above all else, and this stopped him from coming across as conceited. He kept an eye out for his sister and imposed his fair rules on his cousins. He demanded courage and loyalty from his friends. Those who took no risks, who couldn't meet his standards of fearlessness, were worthy of his contempt, for ever. No-one could tell where such assertiveness came from. Unless, of course, it was the mountains that had instilled a toughness in him. We'd often observed it: people are, first and foremost, born to a place and that place is a parent to them too.

That evening in the courtyard, the eldest son sat upright, chin quivering, as he listened to his father. He tried to call upon the knightly codes of valour deep inside him, but he had no need to clench his fists in readiness for a fight. The father explained that their little brother was probably blind. Medical appointments had been made: the family would know what they were dealing with in the next couple of months. They had to consider this blindness as an opportunity; the firstborn and his sister would be the only ones at school to know how to use braille playing cards.

The veil of worry that had fallen over the children quickly lifted at the prospect of this newfound fame. Presented in such a way, the ordeal had some appeal. Who cared if the boy was blind? They'd be the king and queen of the playground. There was a logic to this in the firstborn's mind. He already had a reputation for being a leader who was sure of his looks and poise, and his brooding remoteness only heightened his aura. He therefore spent the whole of dinner bargaining with his sister to be the first to show the playing cards to his class. The father tried to get them to agree, joining in the charade he'd initiated. No-one had fully understood yet that a fault line had appeared. Soon the parents would view these days as the last untroubled period of their life. Freedom from worry is a perverse notion. It can only be savoured once it is lost, once it has become a memory.

The parents quickly realised the baby wasn't able-bodied either. His head fell forward like that of a newborn. He needed another person's hand to hold his neck from behind. His arms and legs dangled loose, devoid of strength. If spoken to, the boy didn't reach out, reply or attempt to communicate. His brother and sister jingled little bells and waved toys of all colours, but still the baby didn't notice. His eyes remained elsewhere.

"It's like he's passed out with his eyes open," the firstborn told his sister.

"You mean he's dead," she said, despite being only seven years old.

The paediatrician didn't think any of this boded well. He advised them to get a brain scan and consult a renowned specialist. They had to make another appointment and leave the valley to reach the hospital. We lost trace of them at that point as there are no stones like us in town. But we imagined them parking the car and carefully wiping their feet on the mat beyond the automatic doors.

They stood in a room, swaying on the grey rubber linoleum floor, waiting for the consultant. He called them into his office. He had the scan results in his hand. He invited them to sit down. His voice was surprisingly quiet as he delivered his irrefutable verdict. Their child would grow, for sure, but he'd remain blind. He wouldn't walk either. He wouldn't ever speak. His limbs wouldn't react to any command as his brain was not transmitting what was required. He would cry and express his discomfort, as well as his satisfaction, but no more than that. He'd remain an infant for ever. Well, not for ever. The consultant then explained, in an even softer tone, that the life expectancy of such children rarely went beyond three years.

The parents glanced back over their existence and understood that, from that point on, everything in the future would make them suffer. Everything they'd lived in the past, too; nostalgia for a formerly untroubled time can certainly turn people insane. A rift between a bygone era and a devastating future opened up beneath their feet. Both sides were loaded with pain.

The parents made do with the little courage they had left, though they felt a part of themselves was dying already. In the deepest recesses of their adult souls, a light was dimming. They sat on the bridge, above the river, their hands intertwined, alone and together at the same time, their legs dangling into the void. They wrapped themselves in the noises of the night, like one might wrap oneself in a cape, to keep warm or disappear. They were afraid. "Why us?" they asked themselves. "Why our little boy? Why him?" And, of course: "How will we cope?" The mountains and their valleys made their presence felt in the burbling of waterfalls, in the humming of dragonflies and in the wind.

The slopes around them were made of schist, a stone so brittle it couldn't be carved. Rockslides were what it did best. The locals yearned for the unbreakable granite or basalt found further north, or even the porousness of the limestone up towards the Loire. Yet what stone, other than schist, displayed so many ochre hues and revealed such multilayered, near-liquid textures? That's the way it was: living in the region meant coexisting with chaos. The parents, sitting on the edge of the parapet, knew they'd have to apply this logic to their lives.

The children didn't fully understand what was going on, only that a devastating force they couldn't yet call grief had propelled them into a different world. And this new world was severed from everything they'd previously known. It was a place where their youthful sensitivity would be tested and wounded without anyone coming to their rescue. The days of dreamy innocence were over. They'd have to comb through the rubble of their lives alone. But children of that age still have a basic pragmatism. Regardless of the turmoil around them, they wanted to know when they'd be given their snacks, or when they could go and catch crayfish again. It was June. The baby was six months old. His siblings still had a different perspective on matters. They made a point of thinking: "June means summer is nearly here and our cousins will arrive soon." Indeed, elsewhere, all around them, in the wider world, other babies were being born, babies who could see and touch things with their hands and hold their heads up on their own. New life was being generated regardless of the trials they faced and they saw no injustice in this.

The children remained in this state of mind until winter. The firstborn and his sister even enjoyed the summer although they avoided any discussion about their brother with their cousins. They preferred not to think about their exhausted parents and their awkward attempts at carrying the baby from the rocker to the sofa, and from the sofa to the big cushions in the courtyard. When a new school term started, the firstborn and his sister set off to make new sets of friends, their lives structured by trips to school and back.

*

Christmas wasn't ruined. It was always a particularly special occasion for mountain families. And, once again, car doors opened and slammed as the hamlet became the meeting point for the whole valley. Visitors entered the courtyard laden with provisions, treading gingerly on the frozen slate-specked ground. Their loud greetings released little puffs of warmth into the cold air, visible against the metallic black sky. The children festooned garlands of coloured light bulbs along the wall to guide the guests to the house and placed lamps at our feet. They then wrapped themselves up warmly, grabbed electric torches, and headed up into the mountain to design a landing strip out of tea lights so Father Christmas could see it from the sky. The hearths crackled with fires so intense the youngest guests couldn't imagine they'd ever burn out. Fifteen people, preparing wild boar stew, terrines and onion tarts, piled into the kitchen. The maternal grandmother, a small woman dressed in satin, told them what to do. The cousins stood with their violins and flutes next to the Christmas tree, watching it sag under the weight of decorations. Someone cleared their throat, hummed a note. Many of those present were members of choirs. And although only a few of them were regular churchgoers, they all knew their Protestant songs. It was explained to the young that, contrary to what the Catholics stated (those the elders still called Papists),

Hell didn't exist, and you didn't need a priest to speak to God. To question your faith, they added, was part of believing. Old female relatives with wrinkly faces said that good Protestants stuck to their word, gritted their teeth and kept their thoughts to themselves. Only "loyalty, endurance and decency" were required, they said as they watched over the children. Music and scents wafted up into the huge beams, seeped through the walls and spilled down into the courtyard. It wasn't that different from the gatherings of old when the people of the region huddled around fires and pressed themselves up against the sheep they herded indoors whenever it got too cold.

The baby was sitting in the rocker chair, beside the fireplace. He was the only fixed point in the tremendous commotion of the room. He was sniffing the air from the kitchen with the hunger of a small animal, the occasional trace of a smile on his face. Certain noises (the tuning of violins, the knock of a dish against the oak table, a deep voice, the yapping of a dog) triggered a slight clenching of his fingers. His head was turned to one side, his cheek against the fabric of the seat as his neck could bear no weight. His eyes, fringed with long dark lashes, swerved gently from side to side with great solemnity. He seemed both attentive and absent, and as floppy as before although he'd grown. His hair had become a thick mop. His parents, too, had changed.

Further small shifts occurred that Christmas Eve. The firstborn took to staring at the boy in his rocker chair. Why at that particular moment, we don't know. Was it because his brother's disability could no longer be ignored? Was it because the firstborn had become disillusioned with how the world was failing to measure up to his high ideals? Had he singled out his brother as a possible companion – peaceful, loyal, true to himself – someone who wouldn't let him down? Or was it perhaps because the firstborn had finally become aware of his family's situation and his principles were compelling him to take care of the weak and feeble? The fact remains that the firstborn leaned over, wiped the boy's mouth, stroked his head and straightened his back. He then kept the dogs at bay, demanded quiet from those around him, and stopped playing with his cousins and sister. No-one could believe it. He'd always been the handsome, slightly hotheaded and sneering boy who kept to himself, aware of his edge over others. He knew how to track wild boar, teach archery and steal quinces. He was the boy who could walk along a river swollen and muddied from a storm, and stride through the shrill night, brushing dangers aside. All he had to do, it seemed, was pull his hood down with a steady hand to prevent the bats – so feared by his sister and cousins – from getting tangled in his thick dark hair. That was the firstborn: stand-offish, regal, coldly confident. A boy, his friends and family thought, who had the silent authority of a ruler.

But the firstborn had stopped suggesting games to play. His sister and cousins flitted around him excitedly, not daring to disturb. He was more silent than usual. He didn't stray far from the fire and stoked it continuously to make sure his brother kept warm. He'd wedged a cushion into the rocker chair to raise the boy's head. And as he read his book, he slipped one of his fingers into the boy's clenched fists, because that was how his little brother rested, with both hands gripped tight, like the newborn he'd forever remain. It was a slightly strange sight to behold: the firstborn, aged ten – the picture of good health – lost in contemplation, beside a boy the size of a one-year-old – already odd, but not yet completely bizarre – who sat with his mouth half open, without any hope of communication and totally calm, his black eyes wandering. The physical likeness between the two brothers was startling, though no-one could quite say why this resemblance was so distressing to behold. Whenever the firstborn glanced up from his book, his stare set and gloomy, his long eyelashes made him look like a replica of the baby beside him.

That Christmas Eve set an irreversible process in motion. Over the following months, the firstborn became more and more attached to his little brother. Before, there'd been a life and other people. Now, there was the boy. The brothers' bedrooms were side by side. Every morning, the firstborn would wake before anyone else and place a foot on the terracotta floor, shuddering at its coldness. He'd then push open the door next to his and walk over to the bed with the swirls of white iron, the same bed he and his sister had once slept in before they grew too big and requested better arrangements. The baby, however, wasn't going to demand a thing. He'd stay in that bed for ever. The firstborn opened the window and let in the morning air. He knew how to remove the boy delicately from the bed, with one hand behind his neck, and take him to the changing table. He cleaned and dressed him there, before carrying him carefully down the steps to the kitchen to feed him the compote their mother had prepared the night before. But before all these undertakings, he'd lean over the side of the bed and rest his cheek against the baby's, enthralled by the pale softness of it, and remain in this immobile position, skin against skin. He loved the cream-like plumpness of the boy's cheek, its defencelessness, as if it were asking to be stroked, maybe only by him, the firstborn. The baby's breath rose steadily into the room. Their eyes weren't looking in the same direction, the firstborn knew that, so while he stared at the folds in the bedsheets and at the windows onto the river, the infant was gazing into a vague elsewhere; his eyes locked into a sequence of movements no-one could decipher. This suited the firstborn. He'd be the boy's eyes. He'd tell him about the bed and the window; the white foam on the torrent; the mountains beyond the courtyard with their earth the colour of night-blue slate; the wooden door; the rampart-like wall; us, the stones, with our coppery glint; and the flowers bursting from the big-bellied pots with handles like ears. When he was with the boy, the firstborn discovered that he could be patient. For years, his cool composure had been the best armour to soothe his own worries. He preferred to set situations in motion rather than wait for them to occur. Others followed his lead for this reason as they were dazzled by his clear, unhesitating drive. The truth was that he so feared being subjected to events that he preferred to make them happen. Rather than dread the mayhem of the school playground, the pitch darkness of the mountains at night, and his own fear of swarming bats, he always took matters into his own hands and hurled himself across the courtyard at dusk into the vaulted cellar, making the startled and panicked bats fly in all directions.

Nothing like that worked with the boy. He was just there. And there was nothing to fear as he neither posed a threat, nor promised a future. There was no need for the firstborn to take the lead. Something else inhabited the boy. He was the bearer of a message from far back, from elsewhere, which conveyed the peacefulness of the mountains, the timelessness of stones and water-ways – elements that were fully self-reliant. The boy had surrendered to the laws of the world and their diffi-culties, without defiance or bitterness. He was simply there, as obvious as a fold in the earth. "It is better to stand firm than wait," he seemed to be saying. That was a proverb from the Cévennes. Indeed the boy had no need to fight back.

Above all else, the firstborn liked his brother's disin-terested goodness, his innocence. Forgiveness was built into his nature; he didn't pass judgement. His soul was manifestly unaware of cruelty. His happiness was limited to basics: cleanliness, a full stomach, the softness of his purple pyjamas, a hand on his skin. The firstborn knew he was witnessing purity. He was overwhelmed by it. When he was by the boy's side, he no longer sought to rush at life for fear it might escape him. Life was just there, a breath away, neither cowed nor combative, simply present.

Bit by bit, the firstborn learned to interpret the boy's cries. He knew which one meant he had a stomach ache, which one signified hunger, which one discomfort. He gained a knowledge he should have discovered much later in life. He knew how to change a nappy and how to spoon-feed mushed vegetables. He drew up lists of items that needed purchasing: a new pair of purple pyjamas, nutmeg to add flavour to the purées, another bottle of cleansing liquid. He'd give the lists to his mother who'd comply, a whisper of thanks in her eyes. The boy's calmness when he was warm and smelled good reassured the firstborn. The boy's lips then drew back into a smile of contentment, his eyelashes fluttering, and his voice rose in an increasingly loud and seemingly ancient chant, the sole purpose of which was to indicate a satisfaction of his needs – and, possibly, some acknowledgement of the kindness shown him.

The firstborn would hum little songs as he'd quickly understood that hearing was the only one of the boy's senses that functioned. It became a miraculous way of getting through to him. The boy could not see, speak, or grasp, but he could hear. So the firstborn took to modulating his voice. He described the different shades of green in the landscape in whispers: it was almond-coloured, light, bronze, delicate and shimmering, streaked with yellow, dull and flat. He rustled branches of dried verbena against the boy's ear, and counterbalanced this scraping noise with the swashing of water in a bowl. Occasionally, he'd pry a stone from the wall and throw one of us a short distance away so the boy could appreciate its muffled thud against the ground. He told him about three cherry trees a farmer once carried up on his back from a far valley below. The man had climbed one mountain and gone down another, stooped under the weight of the trees which, logically, shouldn't have been able to grow in a different soil, in another climate. Yet the cherry trees had thrived and become the pride of the valley. Each year, the old farmer handed out his harvest of cherries and people ate them with great solemnity. The trees' white springtime flowers were known to bring good luck, too, and people offered them to the sick. But time went by and the farmer died. The three cherry trees died too. No-one tried to understand why this had happened as the evidence was right there in the abruptly shrivelled branches: the trees had followed the man who'd planted them. No-one had the heart to touch the dried-out, grey trunks as they so resembled gravestones. The firstborn described them to the boy, down to the last knot. Never had the firstborn spoken so much to anyone. The world had become a shifting bubble which enabled everything to be translated into voice or noise. A face, a feeling, the past – all had an equivalence in sound. The firstborn told his brother the story of the mountains where plants grew from rocks. Out there was a wilderness filled with boar and birds, a land which rebelled and reasserted itself every time a low wall, a vegetable garden or a terrace was imposed on it. It would always revert to the natural slant of its slopes, to its vegetation and wildlife. It demanded humility from mankind at all times. "This is your land," the firstborn said, "you have to listen to it."

When Christmas came round again, he scrunched the wrapping paper covering the presents and described the shape and colour of toys which would never be played with. The parents, a little baffled and too busy trying to keep themselves going, left the firstborn to it. Even the cousins eventually gave in to his outpouring of kindness and joined him, describing the toys in a loud voice. After that, they described the sitting room, the house, the family members, until it got so out of hand the firstborn ended up laughing too.

The firstborn gets up while everyone else in the house is asleep. Not yet a young man, no longer a child, he wraps a blanket round his shoulders, and walks into the courtyard to reach the stone wall. He rests his forehead against us. His hands rise above his shoulders. Is it the gesture of someone who feels condemned or is he stroking us? He says nothing as he stands still in the frozen darkness, his face close to us. We inhale his breath.

As the sun comes out, and the mountains seem to dust themselves off, ready to soak up the day's first rays of light, the firstborn heads round the back of the house. The ground rises counter to the river's flow, before breaking into a series of waterfalls. The firstborn treads carefully, carrying the now heavy infant with the wobbly head. He has a bag with a water bottle, a book and a camera which hangs down to his hip. He finds the spot where the earth becomes flatter, where the stones form a small beach. He puts the boy down, one hand supporting the back of his neck. He checks his brother's midriff is straight. He turns the boy's chin so his face is in the shade of a huge pine tree and hears him let out a sigh. The firstborn rubs the pine's needles together to release their lemongrass-like scent and wafts them under his brother's nose. The trees are not native to the region. Their grandmother planted them a long while ago. They've thrived on the mountainside, spread and grown tall. Their majestic size has now become a problem. The family have lost count of the branches that have ended up falling on electricity wires and how many stretches of their land no longer enjoy sunlight. The firstborn sees these pines as misfits. It's no coincidence that he likes to place his brother in their shade.

He loves this spot. Sitting next to the boy, he pulls his knees up to his chest and wraps his arms around them. He reads like this, and when he's finished reading, he no longer speaks. He doesn't describe anything to his brother. The world comes to them. The turquoise dragonflies sizzle as they fly past their ears. The alder trees rake their branches through the water, gathering thick clusters of mud at their tips. The trees have hemmed the water into a corridor. Had he allowed his imagination a free rein, the firstborn could have pictured himself in a room lined with flat stones, with pines for a ceiling. He takes a few photos. The river is calm and clear enough for him to see a carpet of golden pebbles along its bed. Further upstream, the water's surface creases and hurtles forward in a white boiling froth, crashing into calm pools, which drain away into waterfalls. The firstborn listens to the rush of the river, overlooked by a bank of ochre and green trees whose branches beckon like hands sprinkling flower confetti.

His younger sister often joins them. The two-year age gap between her and the firstborn sometimes feels like twenty. He watches her step into the frozen water, sucking her tummy in, her fingers spread wide. The river laps at her ankles as she crouches to catch insects skimming across the surface, screeching with joy whenever she gets one. She wades, jumps, and builds barrages or small castles out of rocks. She invents stories. She's imaginative in a way that he's not. A stick becomes a sword, the cup of an acorn a helmet. She speaks in half-whispers, fully focused. The sunlight shrouds her very long brown hair. She pushes it away impatiently. The firstborn loves to watch her living. He notices that she no longer needs armbands and that her shoulders no longer burn now that she's started to apply suncream. He remembers the hornets' nest hidden in the tallest pine the previous summer. He gets up, checks, and sits down again. He stays there, his heart jittery but happy, surrounded by those he loves: his sister, his brother and us, the stones, there as both riverbed and playground.

Little by little, the boy recognised the firstborn's voice. He was now smiling, babbling, crying and expressing himself like a newborn though his body had grown. As he was permanently laid flat, and couldn't chew, the roof of his mouth had caved in. His face, as a result, had become more oval and his eyes seemed bigger. The firstborn spent hours trying to follow the black beads of his pupils as they danced lazily from side to side. Never did he think of other children the boy's age and the sort of developmental milestones they would have reached. He didn't compare. Not so much out of a desire to protect his brother, but more because his happiness was complete. Indeed, his happiness was so unusual that any conventional version of it seemed dull to him. He had no interest in it.

The boy was often placed on the sofa, his head supported by a cushion. That was enough for him to seem content. He listened to the world around him. Thanks to his little brother, the firstborn was coming to appreciate both the hollowness and fullness of every hour that passed. He moulded himself to the boy, became like him. He had reached a new level of responsiveness to all things around him: a rustling in the distance, a sudden cooling of the air, the whoosh of a poplar tree, its small leaves flipped by the wind, shining like glitter. It was an appreciation of the substance of every instant, whether it be filled with anguish or joy. It was a language of the senses, of the infinitely small, a science of silence, something that he hadn't been taught anywhere else. This was no ordinary boy, the firstborn told himself, and his knowledge was not ordinary either. His little brother who'd never learn a thing was teaching others.

The family bought a songbird so that the boy could listen to its chirping. They took to turning the radio on, to speaking in loud voices, to opening all the windows, to letting the sounds of the mountains waft into the house so the boy didn't feel alone. The house would then echo with the sound of waterfalls, sheep bells, bleating, barking, squawking, thunder and cicadas.

The firstborn didn't loiter when school ended. He ran to the bus and headed home. Thoughts he didn't need to have gathered in his mind: is there any bath soap or saline solution left? Are there enough carrots for a purée?

Are the purple pyjamas dry? He stopped going to his friends' houses. He didn't look at girls, didn't listen to music. He was busy.

The boy turned four. He'd continued to grow and was now harder to carry. They dressed him in pyjamas which looked like tracksuits, with material that was as thick as possible because his lack of movement made him particularly sensitive to the cold. He had to be shifted regularly otherwise his skin broke out in open sores. Despite this precaution, he'd developed a dislocation of the hips from lying down all the time. He didn't suffer any pain from this, but his legs remained bowed and thin, the skin on them almost as translucent as his face. The firstborn, who would massage the boy's thighs with almond oil, had understood the importance of touch. He'd gently unfurl his little brother's tightly clenched fists to place some matter or other in his palms. He brought strips of felt back from school and holm oak twigs from the mountains. He stroked the inside of the boy's wrists with tufts of mint and rolled hazelnuts over his fingertips, speaking to him all the while. On rainy days, he opened the window and stretched his brother's arm outside so he could feel the downpour. He blew softly into his mouth. A miracle often occurred. The boy would break into a smile accompanied by a whimper of delight. It sounded blissful, a touch silly, as it emerged out of silence and grew sharper, becoming clearer and clearer. It was a kind of music, the firstborn thought. Unlike his parents, who stayed awake at night, he didn't wonder what his brother's voice might have sounded like had he been able to speak, what personality he might have had – cheerful or reserved, home-loving or mischievous – or what his gaze might have been like had he been able to see. The firstborn took the boy as he was.

One afternoon in April, during the Easter holidays, the firstborn made the most of one of his parents' shopping trips to take his brother to the local park. It was a green area on the outskirts of town dotted with swings and merry-go-rounds. The worried parents had agreed to the idea with a quick nod and promised to rush in and out of the grocer's as fast as they could. The firstborn extracted the boy from his special car seat. There was an art to the manoeuvre. The boy's bottom had to be resting on one forearm while the other free hand held his neck. The firstborn could feel the boy's breath on him. He was getting considerably heavier. From afar, he looked as though he'd fainted.

The firstborn crossed the road, went through the gate to the park and placed the boy on the grass. He lay down next to him and described the scene in a gentle voice.

The cries from the sandpit, the creaking of the merry-go-round and the far-off echoes from the market enveloped them in noise. The firstborn interspersed his words with the odd kiss on the boy's wrist, keeping an eye out for flies. His fear was that an insect might slip through his lips (he breathed with them open because of the malformation in the roof of his mouth).

A shadow fell over them and, hearing a voice, the firstborn looked up.

"Excuse me – sorry – I feel bad for you. Why are you wasting your time babysitting freaks at your age? Is it to earn extra pocket money?"

The words were well intentioned – as is so often the case, devastatingly so – and had come from a mother. The firstborn half-sat up, leaning on his forearms. The woman wasn't from the area. She didn't appear to be mean.

"But, *Madame*," he said, "he's my brother."

She coughed, embarrassed, and turned to shout a series of children's names into the playground. The firstborn didn't immediately feel any sorrow or anger. The question hadn't seemed malicious. The woman just hadn't understood, that was all. Surely his brother was as entitled to happiness as anyone else.

The firstborn's embarrassment at people staring at the pushchair would come later, triggering feelings of shame, and what felt like a betrayal of his brother. It was how the invisible barrier separating him from *others* and their overbearing normality came to be erected. *Others* meant noisy, triumphant families, stampeding, bursting with deafening life, without consideration for amorphous bodies or caved-in mouths. *Others* were those who leaped out of cars without the need to extricate themselves from special seats. *Others* meant school peers who collapsed into pathetic worrying as soon as they were given a poor grade, not to mention their smiles of unbearable kindness and pity, which made disgust seem preferable. Thousands of such experiences would build up over time and set the firstborn on his path towards loneliness. The mountains, of course, didn't pass judgement. Like the animals who sheltered in them, they were welcoming, a place to escape to. Didn't the word "refuge" come from the word *"fugere"*, to flee? The mountains allowed him to retreat and take a step back from the world. At the same time, he had to accept that he did live amongst *others.* They were the great teeming majority. He couldn't just cut himself off from them. It helped him to view *others* like some sort of trough where he could occasionally quench a need for normality. A birthday party, an archery competition, a dinner with his parents' friends, a trip to the supermarket: all alleviated his loneliness and reminded him that *others* could keep you standing. They gave you a sense of belonging and a feeling that everyone's hearts sometimes beat as one. In the queue at the supermarket, or waiting for food at the school cafeteria, or stepping into a house adorned with balloons, the firstborn could pretend he wasn't different from *others*. Even when the family's shopping trolley was full of nappies, little jars of food and almond oil, he could pretend they had a baby at home. But when his friends asked: "How many siblings do you have?" he said, "Two". And he then came up with a way not to answer the next question: "What year are they in at school?" He learned to outwit *others*. He'd have liked to have said: "Two, and one is disabled". He'd have loved to switch conversations in a natural way. Instead, he felt guilty. The unbearable *others* had that hold over him. They could even force him into making a mistake when he hadn't done anything wrong, like the time the gaudy truck that criss-crossed the valley in the summer came selling chestnut dough-nuts again.

The cousins enjoyed scanning the horizon for the truck's arrival while the adults came out of their houses clutching their wallets. No sooner bought than wolfed down, the doughnuts were short-lived and the children begged for more. The firstborn heard the truck while he was busy in the orchard below the road, by the water's edge, gathering Pippin apples up into a cloth. They weren't edible, as they were full of wormholes and pecked

35

by birds, but it didn't matter. He had moved the rocker seat all the way to the orchard so the boy could feel the battered and dented shape of the fruit in his palms. The firstborn loved the cool air of the area beyond the bridge with its tree trunks wrapped in protective wire meshing. No passing car could see them there as they were lower than the road. But the firstborn did raise his head and hear the truck's engine as it got closer, and he saw it passing above him with a swarm of cousins in hot pursuit. What was he to do? Should he stay there and miss out on the doughnuts? Unthinkable. Or quietly walk back up the hill, weighed down by the sagging boy? He couldn't do that either. Without thinking, he rolled the apples out of the cloth, flicked it clean and placed it over the boy. He then rushed up the orchard slope, reached the road, crossed the bridge and charged towards the truck without glancing back.

He mingled with his excited cousins, helped his sister unwrap her doughnut, smiled like the rest of the children and didn't dare turn his head towards the orchard. His doughnut tasted like cardboard.

When the truck set off down the road again, he slipped away and started to run. He nearly slid over on the gravelly slope down to the orchard. He saw the grass, the dancing shadows of the branches and the frame of the rocker chair with the apples scattered around it. Then, he saw the white cloth, with dark hair poking out beneath it and two clenched fists sticking out either side. The boy wasn't crying. Instead he was concentrating on the soft fabric which had suddenly covered his face. He'd been able to breathe as his head was leaning to one side. The firstborn knelt down, a lump in his throat, pulled the cloth away and straightened the boy's head. He then rested his cheek against his brother's and whispered "sorry" over and over. The boy made no sound, merely blinked, bothered by the warm, salty drops trickling onto his face.

Back in those days, around the time when the woman accosted him in the town park, the firstborn hadn't fully realised the harm others could inflict with their stupidity and tyranny. He was learning to let go of things which, like the doughnut truck, he didn't care for anyway. His new goal was to behave like the mountains: to protect. His life was filled with worries of all kinds. He had to touch his brother's hands and check their temperature; rearrange his sister's scarf; warn her not to go near the twitchy *Raïoles,* the ewes that often streamed along the side of the roads. One day when she brought home an almost-dead dormouse, he told her to chuck it in the river. The overly protective attitude he displayed towards his sister would later stop him from having children of his own. Those who shudder at the slightest noise, who constantly fear the worst, don't make for stable parents. Yet that was the price to pay, he thought. Protecting was his mission, as deeply ingrained in him as the ochre was in the ridged stones of the mountains. When the giant cedar near the mill was chopped down, the adults tried in vain to gather the children together for the event, but they were nowhere to be found. The firstborn, fearing a branch might wound his sister, had taken her to a different part of the mountains to pick wild asparagus. They spent the morning together bent over, scouring the ground for spindly shoots. The firstborn was punished, but he refused to apologise. He knew he'd done the right thing. Cutting a tree down was dangerous and he'd been right to keep his sister away. It was blindingly obvious: life's happiness could be felled in one go – the way a childhood could topple abruptly into the unknown, a body give up responding, and parents suffer. One day, his teacher asked him what job he wanted to do later in life and he replied, "Older brother".

His sister, on the other hand, seemed carefree. She was as lively as she was pretty. From time to time, she dressed the boy up as if he were a doll. The firstborn scowled at this and removed the make-up, lace hat and bracelets. Yet he didn't resent his sister. He found her vivaciousness comforting. The chaos she whipped up did him good. It was a change from his other sibling who was laid out like an old man. He drew from her the joy he could no longer find in himself. The girl didn't seem to grasp the reality of the situation. She persisted in asking endless questions, throwing tantrums and getting carried away by the stories she invented. She continued to be a child. He envied her this sweet innocence until the day a girl from a nearby hamlet came to play in the courtyard. The girl pointed her chin at the firstborn and asked the sister if she had other siblings. No, she said, she didn't.

The nursery on the edge of town, which looked after the boy during the week, told the parents it could no longer provide for him. The place catered to the needs of disadvantaged children, such as those who were waiting to be rehoused or assessed, sometimes the partially disabled, but certainly not the severely disabled like their son. The staff had neither the necessary equipment nor the requisite training. The boy had recently developed shaking fits in which his eyes blinked fast and his hands jerked around. Minor epileptic fits, the consultant had reassured the family. They weren't painful, and they could be treated with a few drops of Rivotril. But the fits were dramatic enough to frighten the nursery staff. The boy had also swallowed things down the wrong way on more than one occasion, and the women on duty panicked at his coughs, unsure of what to do. Not to mention that there was the risk of a flu epidemic which could floor a body as fragile as his. *Some place* had to be found for him elsewhere. "Aren't there agencies or specialised institutions?" the parents asked. "Not really," they were told, "not locally." People in the area preferred dealing with normal things, the kind that didn't cause trouble. They didn't much go for people who were different. They had nothing planned for them. Schools refused to take them on; the transport system wasn't equipped for them. The local roads and pavements were more like traps. The region didn't seem to care that, for some people, a flight of steps, a kerb or a pothole felt like cliffs, a great wall and a bottomless pit. So forget about a specialised unit for children who didn't fit in . . . We, the stones, caught snippets of conversation and heard worried voices filled with questions as they drifted through the open door into the courtyard. Over the years, we'd witnessed many such moments of utter loneliness. And the parents were indeed alone. They became accustomed to driving into town to get never-ending administrative processes underway. They left the house early, walked up to the small parking area and got into the car. They'd take two sandwiches and a bottle of water. These trips could last the whole day. In town-hall offices, in social service centres, and in ministry departments supposedly designed to help families such as theirs, they felt as if they were being pushed further underwater; the challenges they faced only grew bigger and bigger. The path ahead was cold and inhuman, littered with acronyms of all kinds: MDPH, ITEP, IME, IEM, CDAPH. The people they met were either absurdly procedural or despicably apathetic. The parents discussed it late at night in hushed tones. They had to comply with so many ludicrous rules. They had to stand in grey rooms where a jury would decide whether or not they were eligible for an allowance, an application, an official label, a *place* somewhere, if they were lucky. They had to prove how their finances had changed since the boy's birth, and prove his needs, too, with the back-up of medical certificates and neuro-psychometric assessments, all carefully stored in a folder that became more precious to them than their wallets. They were asked, too, to draw up a life plan, even though not much of a life remained. They met other parents like them: broken, strapped for cash because their subsidies hadn't come through in time, or others horrified that one department hadn't transmitted their case file to another – and that in the event of moving house, the whole application had to be filed all over again. They discovered there was a requirement, every three years, to prove that a child was still disabled ("Because you think his legs will have regrown in that time?" they overheard one mother scream at an official). They saw other parents collapse as their child was evidently not maladapted enough to be granted any help, and yet too maladapted to be given a place in a mainstream school. The mother had stopped working to look after the boy, since no-one else would. The parents discovered there was a vast no man's land on the margins of society, filled with people who lived without any healthcare, strategy or support. They learned, too, that mental disease, being sometimes invisible, added an extra layer of difficulty. "Does my daughter have to be physically deformed for you to get your arses in gear?" a father rasped in a health centre that only opened for a few hours each morning. More than once, the firstborn saw his exhausted parents get up early and come back empty-handed, with more papers and forms to fill in, before setting off again to join queues in the hope of getting some certificate; to be put on hold while on the telephone; to be forced to challenge a date or a mistake – in truth, he thought, to become supplicants. It was enough for him to develop a burning hatred of all things administrative and official. It was the only negative emotion to anchor itself in him permanently. As an adult he was unable to handle queues for office counters or reception desks. He hated contracts and filling out application forms. He'd never renew his cards or his subscriptions, preferring to pay fines and added fees rather than deal with anything remotely bureaucratic even for a second. He wouldn't apply for visas or go to a notary or enter a courtroom, preferring not to buy a car or an apartment. No-one ever understood this mental block, except his sister who knew how to negotiate tax deductions, how to cancel a telephone contract and settle a health insurance bill. The firstborn had to challenge this fear when renewing his identity card as it required his physical presence. His sister always booked the appointments, filled in the paperwork, and accompanied her brother without saying a word as he sat, tense and sweating on a plastic chair in the waiting room, wishing he could run away.

The exhausted and sad parents understood they had to consider all the alternatives. They looked as far afield as possible for something more specialised and even thought about paying more. They considered the possibility of sending their boy abroad, to a country where atypical children weren't simply thought of as a burden. They gave up, however, as the idea of having their son so far from home distressed them. At night-time, in the courtyard, the mother wiped her eyes and smoked cigarettes while the father replaced her tisane with wine.

*

They were told about a care home in the middle of nowhere, hundreds of kilometres away. It was L-shaped and set in a meadow. Its residents were children like the boy, but they were looked after by nuns. Did the nuns live there or return home at night? Were they from that region? Would they understand that the boy was sensitive to the cold; that scratchy wool clothes bothered him; that he liked carrot purée and the feel of grass on his skin; and that the slamming of doors made him jump? And would the nuns be able to cope with his trembling fits, or food swallowed down the wrong way or his chalazions, the inflammations of the eyelid which seemed to affect him more and more? The firstborn didn't have any answers to these questions. He hated the stoneless, flat landscape around the care home, the mildness of the climate there. He disliked the absurd walls surrounding the building and garden, as if the boy could possibly attempt a quick getaway. The car drove through a blue gate onto a stretch of gravel, which crunched too loudly. The care home appeared squat beneath its tiled roof, the walls white. The firstborn immediately missed the sand-coloured walls of their valley, the distinct slate tone mixed with lime. His heart hurt from the pain of this realisation. He imagined himself snatching the boy from his car seat, turning on his heels and running off into the meadows. He was so absorbed by these thoughts that he didn't acknowledge the women in white wimples as they lined up to greet the family.

He didn't get out of the car. He refused to visit the premises or to say goodbye. He focused on the noises around him as his little brother had taught him. The hiss of the car boot, the dragging of suitcases from the car – had anyone, he wondered, packed his favourite purple pyjamas or given him a pebble from the river, a stick, something to remind him of his home in the mountains? Then the firstborn heard steps on the gravel, the creaking of a gate, silence, birdsong he didn't recognise, further steps, the slamming of a car door, the stutter of an engine. He finally opened his black eyes as meadows shot past and he went back to his former life.

His father laughed about the nuns when the cousins rang and teased them about their unfortunate interaction with the "Papists". Everyone was relieved to know the boy was being taken care of. Everyone except the firstborn.

A pit of sadness grew within him. He avoided the cushions on the sofa still imprinted by the shape of his brother's body. He no longer went to the river or wrote lists. His whole morning routine changed. He lingered at school once the day had ended as no-one needed new nappies or carrot purée.

He cut his hair and started wearing glasses. He threw

himself into his secondary-school studies with the utmost seriousness one might expect of a young man whose mind was overspilling with memories and thoughts. His peers observed him – the same *others* who'd created a barrier between the world and his brother. He had to put up with them. He knew that. He included them in his life, just enough so as not to be left out, but not enough to open up fully to them or to get close. By mingling with different year groups, he always found someone to have lunch with in the cafeteria and even went to a few parties. He avoided being on his own although he was a loner. Everything was calculated, a façade. In the morning, he woke in tears, as the moment he opened his eyes he heard the rush of the river and then remembered the small empty bed without sheets in the room beside his. So his heart hardened and he could feel it shrivel and turn into a compact, heavy mass, which moments later would explode, splintering the day ahead into thousands of jagged pieces. He touched his chest and was surprised not to find himself bleeding. If he couldn't breathe properly, he stood still and leaned his torso forward, his bare feet on the tiled floor. When he plucked up enough courage, he walked past his brother's bedroom and acknowledged the emptiness of the bathtub. At the edge of the sink, he spotted the flask of almond oil which no longer served any purpose.

Wherever he went, he had to endure the boy's physical absence. That was the hardest part: not being able to touch his pale soft skin and place a cheek against his. Not being able to smell him, feel the texture of his hair and see his wandering black eyes. He missed the act of lifting his little brother, both hands under his armpits, his body on his chest, his breath on his neck. Then the scent of flower blossom. And the quiet immobility, that gentleness which had helped him live. He also had to face the constant worry of not knowing if the boy was being looked after properly. He was terrified he might be cold – particularly that while he, the firstborn, was doing his homework, sitting on a bus or picking the first figs of the year, at that precise moment, the boy might be cold. The overlapping of these two periods in time seemed unbearable to him. He worried, too, that the inexperience of his carers could harm him further. He often retreated to the orchard where he'd once laid a cloth over his brother and just stared at the fallen apples in the grass. He knew it was pointless to stand there, frozen by memories, but he couldn't do anything about it. It was a way of calming the runaway beat of his heart. It made the boy feel close again.

One day the parents took the firstborn to a cousin's wedding. He didn't like crowds; even less did he like smart clothes and the conventions of politeness. Yet he knew how to put on a brave face when needed, and his parents seemed happy. His mother had straightened her hair for the occasion and smiled whenever his father cosied up to her. Sitting around a table, in a stretch of long grass with the mountains in the background, the firstborn felt he was living in a moment of reprieve – for people like him, events such as weddings were a kind of truce. He searched for his sister and spotted her playing on some outdoor gym equipment under the trees. Suddenly a sentence rang out around him, something like: "Love is not just looking at each other, it's looking in the same direction." The best man had said it into the microphone. It was exactly the sort of sentence that always got dredged up at weddings. It was, apparently, a quote by Antoine de Saint-Exupéry. The firstborn found it idiotic. It made marriage sound like teamwork. What a strange world, he thought, where love had to be given a goal. What a pity no-one understood that to love was, in fact, to drown in the eyes of another, even if those eyes were blind. The firstborn felt very alone. He glanced around him. The guests were listening to the speech. He'd have given anything then to have his brother with him. He'd have laid him down in the grass and looked straight into his eyes. He remembered the shock he'd felt when his French teacher made them read the romance of Tristan and Iseult. What if those two had been told to "look in the same direction"? They'd melded one into the other, that's exactly what they'd done, and although the firstborn preferred maths to literature, he'd grown fond of those lovers. He'd understood all too well how love could fuel a contempt for rules.

The firstborn's sensitivity to sound made him jump at the slightest noise at school. He hated the stampeding of feet in the corridors, the jibes the pupils yelled at each other when assembling by the gates. Although he didn't show it, the loud commotion often brought tears to his eyes because then he longed for the sweet presence of another, his silence and steady breath. It's me, he thought, who is maladapted. The idea that his brother was on his own in a faraway place, that he existed elsewhere, brought about a pain so vivid that he developed methods for fending it off. He stopped reading altogether and focused on the sciences. They, at least, didn't hurt or open up pathways to memory, didn't deliberately seek out feelings. The sciences were like the mountains. They were simply there, whether you liked it or not, oblivious to sorrow. There was an accuracy to them. They set their own laws. They were either right or wrong, come stillness or storm. The firstborn, therefore, immersed himself in questions of geometry, in wordless puzzles and sequences which unfolded like a primitive language. He needed cold and calming evidence. If he looked up from his work for too long, he felt an angry jealousy towards the nuns. He couldn't control it so he dived back into his numbers.

Years later he'd come to understand that the nuns had reached an astounding level of non-verbal communication. They could interact without words or gestures. They'd understood that special form of love, the finest, most mysterious and elusive form there is, one that relies on sharpened animal instincts, on anticipating, giving, filling oneself with gratitude for the present, without needing a thing in return. They were like stones: filled with some sort of innate peace, untouched by worries.

At the start of each school holiday, the family travelled down from the mountains and headed to the care home in the meadow to fetch the boy. The firstborn saw the blue gates in the distance and waited for the sound of the gravel without getting out of the car. The nuns came down the front porch with the boy in their arms. They kept his head upright and patiently strapped him into the special seat in the back of the car. All the while, the mother stroked his head and thanked the women. The firstborn looked straight ahead. His heart was beating away in the pit of his stomach, inside his fingers and temples. He thought his whole body might detonate. He could smell a new scent – not the orange blossom he knew, but a sweeter fragrance. He wanted to lean into his brother's neck and place his cheek against his, a sensation he'd craved for too long. So he removed his glasses to resist the desperation of that urge: he was so shortsighted there was no risk of him seeing his brother next to him. Seeing his brother would start the process of separation all over again. It would mean reliving all those days without him, without the softness of his skin and his smile. It would make the boy's return to the care home in the meadow even more painful the next time round. It would deal a hammer blow to the progress he'd made in building up his courage. It would mean lying down on the ground and dying.

So he kept his glasses off throughout the ride home, gritting his teeth all the way. He kept his head turned towards the window, as if in a fog. Green, white and brown flashes shot past. For one fleeting second, he gave in and looked at the seat by the opposite window. He was relieved that he couldn't see much, except perhaps for the boy's thin calves which now stuck out even further. What did he have on his feet? Slippers, maybe, but where had they come from? He turned his head back again, avoiding his sister's glares, focusing instead on the flashes of colour outside, rubbing his burning eyes.

His mother changed the boy's nappy at a service station on the motorway, fed him, and muttered something in his ear. It reassured the firstborn to know his brother was being spoilt. But still he refused to look at him for fear of being engulfed by emotion.

When they reached the courtyard at home, the sister bounded in first. She was no longer a little girl, though she remained just as playful and lively. Recently, she'd had her eye on her elder brother. It was her turn to watch over him. The firstborn walked into the courtyard with nothing in his arms. The mother was carrying the boy, treading carefully. He'd grown. The distance between his bottom and his shoulders had got bigger and his head still had to be kept upright without twisting it too much. The mother placed the boy on the large cushions while she opened up the house. At that point, we, the stones, saw the firstborn pull up a plastic chair some distance from his brother, sit down and squint. He was trying to work out where the boy was. He hadn't put his glasses back on as seeing his brother was still too over-whelming. Yet the drive home had taught him that not seeing him was also too overwhelming. So now he was trying to both see him and not see him at the same time.

This pattern of behaviour carried on throughout the holidays. The firstborn would settle somewhere in the courtyard with the excuse of finishing his maths home-work and then look up, eyes like slits, jaw tense, and try and make out the boy's stretched-out body. He no longer fed him, no longer spoke to him, no longer touched him. But, as he rinsed his hands longer than necessary in the sink, he'd always turn his head towards the bath-tub and observe his mother washing the boy. And when he peeled vegetables next to the sofa, pausing to look up every so often, his whole being seemed on edge and channelled towards a single aim, one promise he'd made to himself: he wouldn't lean over and press his cheek against the boy's.

The firstborn's shortsightedness meant he only ever saw a hazy outline of his brother. He had to rely on his hearing instead. He knew how to do that. He listened to his brother breathe and sputter, swallow his spit, then sigh and whimper. At night, the firstborn would wake with a start, troubled by images in his mind. He'd throw back the sheets, step onto the terracotta floor and open the boy's door, just enough to make out the vague swirls of the bed in the other room. He didn't go any further. He simply listened to the boy breathing. He absolutely wouldn't get any closer. He knew he wouldn't have got over it. So he stayed in the doorway, shaking, broken. It was absurd. But that's how it was. His life had to take a different shape.

At night, he goes and leans against the stone wall in the courtyard. He rests his forehead on us, his hands at the level of his face, and presses down, his body tense, ready for a showdown.

Months later, in the summer, the firstborn, now nearly a young man, tied up the strings on his rucksack and set off to meet friends in another part of the region. The trip was meant to last several days. After he'd said goodbye to his parents and crossed the courtyard, we saw him turn round and retrace his steps. It shouldn't have surprised us. Nothing lasts for ever. Even we'll end up as dust. The time had come for the firstborn to rekindle his bond with the boy. Had his imminent departure prompted this? Had the pain of those months away from his brother been too much to bear? Or was it a newfound maturity, a weariness, even, that had come from not being able to reason with himself? Regardless of the cause, a certainty took root in the firstborn as he readied himself to leave the courtyard: living *side by side* with his brother was no longer possible. He'd tried. He'd taken his glasses off, made new friends and filled his days, often with nothing more than mere existence. He'd fought as hard as he could to settle for little more than a hazy outline of his brother. He'd even managed not to go and lean over the boy's bed on nights he couldn't sleep. Yet it had all been in vain. He could only conclude that living *side by side* was not possible. He put down his rucksack and climbed the stairs.

His footsteps took him to the room. Pushing the door open, he marched up to the bed with the white swirls. The boy was lying on his back as usual. He'd grown. He was wearing wool-lined slippers and a purple-coloured pair of pyjamas that would have fitted a ten-year-old. His fists were clenched, his mouth half open. He was as he'd always been. His black eyes still roamed the room, though they could also have been following distinct pathways. He was listening to the river and the cicadas through the open window. The firstborn gripped the swirls of the bed frame like a handrail and bent down. The boy had his head turned towards the window, as if his round, silky cheek were being offered up to his elder brother. The firstborn settled on it the way a mother bird returns to her nest, with such relief that tears welled up in his eyes. The buried words from the past months bubbled to the surface. He was speaking to his brother like before, effortlessly, their cheeks touching, his voice taking on a particular intonation. He told the boy about how the trick of taking his glasses off so as not to see him, while also trying to do so, had failed, and then about the endless tunnel of days without him. The firstborn's heart split open like a fruit. But the boy wasn't smiling. He wasn't even blinking. He was looking elsewhere, breathing gently as he'd always done. He no longer recognised his elder brother's voice. How long had it been since he'd spoken to him? The firstborn stood up, the blood draining from his face. He grabbed his bag and went to join his friends.

He lasted four days. On the fifth day of his time away, at dawn, he hitchhiked back home from the edge of a chestnut grove. By the afternoon, he was shoving the wooden gate open with his shoulder. He crossed the courtyard with soldier-like pace, startled his parents in the sitting room, and headed straight up the stairs. Nothing had changed in four days: the bed, the mosquito net by the open window bathed in sunlight, the growling of the river. He opened the door wide and leaned down into the bed, out of breath. He spoke in his hesitant, stuttering voice, putting the dread that he'd been forgotten by the boy to one side. He cried as he'd done years before in the orchard, wetting his brother's face, kissing his fingers. He asked for forgiveness. The boy fluttered his long, black eyelashes and stretched out his mouth. A thread of happy sound emerged, toneless except for the last note, which soared into the room lighter, even more ethereal.

The firstborn announced that he'd spend the rest of the summer at home.

Fully embracing his reunion with his brother, he took a bowl full of warm water into the courtyard along with a pair of scissors and a comb. He kneeled down by the cushions, gently splashed the boy's head and used a towel to dab his hair. He then cut the hair on one side, took hold of the boy's cheeks with both hands, turned his face, and cut it on the other side. He stroked rather than wiped his face afterwards. The gestures were coming back to him, unchanged. He needed time, though, and the summer holidays only lasted two months. When they drove back to the care home in the meadow, the firstborn didn't get out of the car or say goodbye.

Returning to school didn't trouble him as much as in previous years. He felt his brother was safe and that he, himself, was on a path of his own towards a future of some kind. For the first time, these two facts weren't at odds. The firstborn could imagine the nuns without resentment. They were taking good care of the boy. It reassured him. He recalled the babbling voice in the bed with the swirls and drew strength from it. He gave his maths exercises a break, listened to music instead, went to the cinema and joined in conversations at school. He knew, of course, that he'd never be as cheerful as his happy-go-lucky friends; he didn't have their self-assurance. He carried a list of topics for conversation on him at all times for fear of not having enough to say, in case a prying question threw him off track. He didn't like to be unsettled or feel exposed. He wouldn't let his guard down too much; he'd forbidden that. The price to pay was too high. No-one would pierce the block of worry inside him even though he was sometimes able to open up. He'd even get the giggles at times, loosen his grip, and allow himself to have a little crush or two. That was all he could afford. When he thought of his brother, he smiled. The boy was both far away and always with him. He sensed him in the hurried swishing of a grass-snake in the water, in the air thick with powdery white flowers, in the rising wind, in the swaying trees along the river. Beauty would always be indebted to his brother. His awareness of this became like armour, a protective muscle. The prospect of seeing his brother during the school holidays no longer sent his heart into an out-of-control spin. Quite the opposite: it lifted him and gave him the determination to keep his glasses on, to make the most of the boy's presence. He couldn't wait to rediscover his stillness. This was a new and powerful feeling. What had previously been an ordeal had finally become a strength. The firstborn could now appreciate his brother's gift to the full: maladapted as he was, he had the power to bestow strength on others. And the mere fact of his existence granted that. Even if the firstborn had lost the habit of confiding in others, of opening up to them, of inviting friends over to his house, he'd received this precious love instead. So for the first time, he decided he would get out of the car when they arrived at the care home in the meadow and maybe even chat with the nuns.

He'd reached this point in his rebirth when he was told the boy had died. As quietly as he had lived, the nuns said. The firstborn would now never get to speak to them. The boy's fragile body had simply given up, surrendered, from a lack of breath, without a struggle. There was a flu epidemic lurking. His coughing and epileptic fits had got worse, become more frequent, and he'd been swallowing with greater difficulty. Meals had been taking longer. He'd fought as best he could, had coped with what he had. It seemed as if the inner resources he'd always drawn on had dried up. One morning he hadn't woken up.

The nuns were wiping their eyes. The boy's body was waiting for the family in a room at the back, near the laundry. There was the usual flurry of sounds, then whispers, as well as footsteps on a tiled floor. The firstborn didn't understand any of it; his movements were now mechanical. He could only think that he was stepping for the first time into the place where his brother had lived. The corridors smelled of warm mashed potato. The beds, hemmed in by tall, detachable bars, reached halfway up the walls. The firstborn noticed how there weren't any cushions or stuffed toys, which he thought was perhaps a sensible precaution. The bed covers were a pale yellow. On the walls, he spotted posters of ducklings, chicks and kittens. There were no children's drawings, he thought, because none of the residents could hold a pencil. The windows looked out onto the garden. Had anyone ever opened the windows so his brother could hear the noises outside? He thought that maybe they had.

As he entered the room, the firstborn took off his glasses and shut his eyes. His hand felt a hard rim which he assumed was the edge of the coffin. He bent forward and his nose met the cold, soft surface of the boy's cheek. He opened his eyes for a few seconds and caught sight of the boy's closed, translucent eyelids, criss-crossed by tiny blue streaks. The eyelashes cast a shadow on the pale skin. The mouth no longer released a single puff of peaceful breath, of course. The boy's knees had been bent slightly, but because of his particular anatomy they were touching the edges of the coffin. His arms had been brought down onto his chest, his fists clenched. The firstborn asked if he could take the purple pyjamas home with him.

Back at the hamlet, dressed in her nightgown, the mother rested her chin on her husband's shoulder and swayed against him. They held each other tight before buckling and falling to the floor. The sister held on to her bedroom windowsill and stared at the mountains beyond the courtyard until the first glow of dawn emerged. The firstborn did nothing. For the first time in years he didn't get out of bed in the middle of the night to lean his head against us in the courtyard.

A lot of people came to the funeral, even though, of course, the boy hadn't really known any of them. They came for the parents, in an open-hearted way. The courtyard was packed. Slowly, everyone walked up the mountain as the dead in these parts are buried deep inside their slopes. The family had its own small cemetery: two big white tombstones in the ground, surrounded by railings, some adorned with curlicues that reminded the firstborn of the boy's bed. The cousins set up some foldable canvas stools, positioned a cello in the grass and got out their flutes. The music wafted upwards.

When it was time to commit the body to the earth, the small crowd stepped back to leave the firstborn alone. He didn't notice. The ropes were let down carefully. As the coffin sank deep inside the mountain, he was shot through by a fear so sharp that it felt more like a bite: "Let's hope he doesn't get cold," he thought.

His eyes were riveted on the loose earth steadily burying the coffin. Aware he was saying his final goodbye, the firstborn made the boy a silent promise: "I'll leave a trace of you."

The consultant, who'd made the initial diagnosis and followed the boy for eight years, had come to the funeral. The boy had lived much longer than expected, he said. His added years of life were proof, if any were needed, that medicine couldn't explain everything. It was no doubt down to the love the boy had received, he told the parents.

From this moment on, the firstborn lives without connection to others as he deems it too dangerous to tie himself to people. Those he loves can easily disappear. He becomes an adult who associates happiness with the possibility of its loss. Good luck or misfortune, it doesn't matter: he won't give life the benefit of the doubt. He's lost all sense of peace. He's one of those people who carries a precise moment in time in their heart, suspended there for ever. Something in him has become stone, which doesn't mean that he's numb – more that he's resilient, steady, unflinchingly the same, one day to the next.

He carries within him, too, a permanent alertness. When he comes out of a meeting, even out of a cinema, and switches his mobile back on, he's hit by a rush of relief. He hasn't received a panicked message. There has been no great upheaval or catastrophe. Fate hasn't snatched someone dear to him and his family is well. If someone is five minutes late, if a bus brakes abruptly, or if he hasn't seen his neighbour in a few days, he feels a tension mount inside him. Worry has planted itself in him. It grows like a mountain fig tree, stubborn and hardy. Perhaps it'll pass. Perhaps not.

He sits upright in bed, in the hollow darkness of the night, his neck damp with sweat, head brimming with images of the boy, worried that something bad has happened to him. He'd like to check he's alright, but he remembers that the boy is no longer with them. Each time, he's stunned by the vividness of his nightmares, as if no time has passed. It's as if his brother has died the day before. He's been told that time heals. In truth, as these nights reveal to him, time mends nothing – quite the opposite. He digs away at the pain, reawakening it, strengthening it a little more each time. Sorrow is all that's left of the boy. He can't escape it – to do so would mean losing the boy for good.

The firstborn gets up and eats a little. He looks out of the window at the dark buildings. They're more silent than the mountains at night. He's taken time to get used to living in the city. For a long time he was appalled by the dogs on leads, and the silent summers, devoid of cicadas and toads. Instinctively, in March, he looks into the skies to see the first swallows. And in July, he listens out for the swifts. He used to wait for the smell of dung, verbena, mint, the sound of sheep bells, the river, the hum of insects and the wind scraping at bark. Though he's known nothing but steepness, he's grown accustomed to flatness, to ground that bears no trace of footsteps, to the sight of women in high heels. His knowledge is ill-adapted to city life. What point is there in knowing that chestnut trees won't survive above an altitude of eight hundred metres, or that hazelnut trees have the supplest wood for making a bow and arrow? No point at all, but he's used to that. He knows what it means to have irrelevant knowledge.

In front of his window, at night, he thinks of the soft tips of the alder branches skimming the river, and of turquoise dragonflies. He invariably ends up reaching for his favourite photo, the one he's had blown up and framed. It's of the river at home and he studies it carefully. He'd almost lain flat on the stones to take it at the same height as the boy's head. His big black eyes are about to swerve blankly away, but in the photograph one could almost think that he's staring back. The wind has flattened his thick hair. His plump cheeks are asking to be stroked. The pine trees tower over them from a distance. The water is flowing fast, sparkling, studded with his sister's little heels as she perches on a ridge of pebbles, her head turned towards the camera, glaring directly at the lens. The blue lacework of the sky is pushing through the foliage and branches. The firstborn could list every single detail of the photo into the small hours of the morning.

Then he sets off for work again.

He's developed a strong mathematical mind: he manages the finance department of a firm. Numbers don't fail him; they're reliable. They don't pull any surprises. Every morning he puts on a dark suit and takes the bus with other men in dark suits. He doesn't like people, but he tolerates them. He has no close allies within his firm. He's friendly with a handful of colleagues – enough of them for him not to sit alone in the cafeteria at lunchtime and to be invited out on Sundays. He knows what he has to say and do to slip by unnoticed. He doesn't inspire mistrust or sympathy. He's a thirty-year-old like any other, an anonymous figure in the crowd. This suits him fine as he has some wild hope that fate will forget about him and leave him alone. No-one understands that he masters calculations, charts, columns of cost-benefit analysis, complex banking transactions and balanced accounts precisely because he once fell prey to arbitrary forces. No-one can guess that behind this besuited manager lies a strange little brother with dancing eyes.

He has no partner, no children. He's left these tasks to his sister. She'll have three girls who will charge around the courtyard screaming during the holidays. She now lives abroad. In another country, with a husband, and children. She's found normality faraway. She's made a point of mending the break in their lives while he's remained a prisoner of it. Perhaps, though, that's a lesson she's learned from watching him. After all, isn't that his role, to walk ahead, to show others what not to do?

We, the guardians of the courtyard, watch over these new children with the same attentiveness as the parents who have since moved to the other house on the river. Once again, we recognise the scrape of the heavy door, the sighs of relief after long car journeys, the garden furniture being dragged outside. We watch the family having dinner, cherishing the ancient rhythm of a new generation taking root. We know that when the sister arrives the firstborn usually isn't far behind. They've stayed close. She gives him papers to sign, warns him of deadlines, of a possible rebate, of the need to renew a contract. She urges him to get out, to make friends. He smiles. He says he's absolutely fine as he is. And we believe him. Wherever he goes, especially in these mountains, he bears the memory of a promise made at the edge of a grave. He leaves a trace of the boy. He sits for hours on the riverbank. We spot his tall silhouette under the pine trees, gazing at the dragonflies and pond skaters. We know his heart is gripped by sorrow. His hand touches the stones where his brother's head used to rest. We feel, however, that something in him is soothed. Sometimes he merely stands still, near to where the cushions were once placed in our shade, listening to the afternoon coming in. When his cousins are there, they reminisce together and laugh about past events. They, too, have had families. He loves to see these children build similar memories to his. He forbids them from going to the mill; repairs a tricycle; insists they wear armbands near the water's edge. Love for him is a form of worry. He'll always be the firstborn.

Come nightfall, he's the last to clear up the courtyard, hosing down the slate stones and watering the hydrangeas. Without fail, he comes over and gently rests his forehead and palms against us. He leans into our warmth, his eyes shut. One evening, his five-year-old niece catches him in this position and asks: "What are you doing?" With a gentle, hidden smile, he says, "I'm breathing."

2

The Sister

SHE RESENTED THE BOY FROM THE MOMENT HE WAS born. Or rather from the moment her mother waved an orange in front of his eyes and realised he couldn't see. The sister's bedroom window looked straight out onto the courtyard. So she'd seen the bright stain of the fruit's colour, her mother crouched down, and heard the faintness of her tender, sing-song voice before it fell silent. She remembered the raging chorus of the cicadas, the tumbling roar of the river, the guffawing of the trees shaken by the wind. Yet nothing remained of that summer sound. There was only her mother's bowed head, an orange in her hand.

The sister understood that a break had occurred at that precise moment. It was all over from then on. Her father could be as upbeat as he liked, promising that they'd be the only ones at school to know how to use braille playing cards, but she wasn't fooled. She could see the veil in his eyes and, above all, his smile, which only started and ended on his lips, while the rest of his face was empty and distant, with no expression of any kind. But her elder brother, the firstborn, had fallen for the great lie. He'd haggled to be the first to take the braille playing cards to school. He'd promised to play with her, only her. And she'd gone along with it. Yet their little brother now reigned supreme.

The boy was draining her family of its strength. Her parents were coping as best they could, but her elder brother had been totally swept up into it. There was nothing left for her. There was no energy to carry her forward.

The more the boy grew, the more he disgusted her. She couldn't admit this to anyone. Born with a weak immune system, always laid out on his back, he was a bundle of endless ailments. Medicine had to be administered through a pipette, his nose wiped, his eyes filled with drops and his head held straight whenever he coughed. Every meal took a good hour. His swallowing was so slow it had to be encouraged by intermittently tipping water from a glass into his partially open mouth, with the constant fear the liquid might go down the wrong way. His skin was so fine it chafed on contact with fabric. It reacted to limestone water, a ray of sunlight and soap. He needed softness, warmth, mushiness – the stuff of newborns and the elderly. The boy, however, fitted neither of these categories. He was stuck midway, a mistake, stranded between birth and decrepitude. A cumbersome, speechless presence, without movement or eyesight. He was, in other words, helpless and exposed. The boy's vulnerability, moreover, provoked fear in those around him, drawing even greater attention to the ills that swamped his body. That is what the sister couldn't bear: the reality of his constantly unhealed wounds. Above all, she hated his inflamed eyelids with the red bumps they called chalazions, which looked like he'd been stung by a wasp. The sticky eyedrops of Rifamycin used to treat him were even more repellent. She had to leave the room when her elder brother applied the buttery gel and gently massaged the boy's eyelids with his index finger.

She didn't like the blackness of his eyes either; the empty pupils gave her the shivers. Then there was his breath, which smelled fetid. Neither did she like his wide-apart, bony white knees. She'd been told that his hip joints no longer worked because he spent so much time flat on his back. They'd come loose from their hinges. It was said, too, that his feet would end up arched like those of a ballerina because they'd never once stepped on firm ground. What was the point of feet, she wondered, if they couldn't walk or support a body?

They put wool-lined leather slippers on his feet. The boy had several pairs. Every time she saw them lying around, she mistook them for dead shrews.

She dreaded bath time. The naked, stretched-out feebleness of the boy's body became more unbearable then. His ribs jutted through the white skin of his frail chest, and he risked drowning if his head rolled to one side. Her elder brother spoke to him softly, as if he were singing a lullaby, commenting on every movement as he held the back of the boy's neck, all the while washing him with his other hand, covering every fold of skin, drizzling it with warm water. Observing the firstborn's profile as he leaned over the bathtub, the sister had to admit the brothers bore a striking resemblance. The contours of their faces were the same, as were their rounded foreheads. They both had thin noses and protruding chins. They had the same slightly narrow black eyes, thick hair, and long, well-defined mouths, too. Indeed, right there before her in the bathroom, she thought, she was seeing the superb original and its botched replica, an unfortunate imitation.

She felt no tenderness towards the boy. To her, first and foremost, he was a sickly puppet who required never-ending care – a perpetual baby.

She'd given up inviting friends over. How could she with such a being in the house? She was ashamed. She'd seen an advert on television with the slogan: "Get rid of all banality in your life." The words had sickened her. She'd have given anything for a bit of banality, to blend into the mass of normal people: two parents, three children, a regular house in the mountains. She dreamed of waking up happy, of an elder brother who was willing to engage with her, of music in the sitting room, of girl-friends staying over on Friday nights. She dreamed of ordinary families with untrammelled lives, of households barely aware of their good fortune.

One day, we saw her cross the courtyard. The boy was lying on his big cushions, lost in his world. A warmth filled the air. It was late on a Wednesday afternoon in September. It would have been the perfect opportunity for the sister's friends to come over and do their home-work with her, for them to eat snacks beside us, perhaps even carve their initials into us, as children like to do in these parts. But that day the sister was brimming with loneliness. So, as she skirted round the big cushions, towards the old wooden gate, she suddenly turned and headed back towards the boy and gave the cushions a kick. They barely shifted as they were enormous garden cushions, more like quilts of impressive weight. The boy didn't blink. The sister, though, had kicked hard. She glanced at the house, fearing she'd been seen, and ran off. We didn't judge her. Who were we to do so? We did, however, recognise that ancient and absurd logic, which is that weakness engenders brutality, and the living like to punish those who aren't alive enough. This logic is specific to humans and animals. It doesn't affect stones.

The sister sank deeper into anger. The boy had cut her off from the world, erected an invisible barrier between her family and others. How could such an impaired being cause so much pain? The boy was destroying her without a sound. With regal indifference, too. Innocence, she was discovering, could also be cruel. She compared the boy to a heatwave pummelling and drying the soil without respite, laying waste to it with relentless fury. The basic laws of the world were without mercy. They did as they pleased. All one could do was stare at the wreckage. The boy had snatched her parents' joy away, thrown her childhood into disarray and stolen her elder brother.

She'd never seen the firstborn so attentive or loving. She was astounded by the changes in him. He'd always been a daredevil, tight-lipped, a little arrogant, ready to lead the cousins up into the mountains, to hunt for bats and hurl clumps of weeds across the river. He was the one who followed wild boar tracks and ate onions raw. She'd always feared and admired him. She'd have followed him anywhere. Now, because of the boy, he no longer noticed her. He hadn't even realised she could swim without armbands. What had happened to the brother she knew? One of his recent preoccupations was checking the chimney flue as he feared the boy might be suffocated by smoke and die. Even the way the firstborn walked had changed. In the days of summer heat, when he went out into the courtyard to move the boy into the shade and rearrange the cushions, his strides seemed supple, oddly slow and purposeful, their pace determined by the draw of those cushions. He was like an animal called back to its litter. She couldn't forgive him for it.

The firstborn, who'd always demanded endurance in others, had sharpened his younger sister's character enough for her to know how to fight back. So she laid claim to her territory. She muscled in while the firstborn read, his finger clasped by the boy's palm, suggesting that the two of them pick blackberries or make a bow and arrow, or take a walk up to the "*drailles*", the mountain paths so narrow hikers couldn't scrape past one another. The firstborn only shot her a questioning glance. Still she pushed ahead. She tried to strike up conversations and force him to engage. She did her best to pry him open. But the firstborn merely answered with a gentle, almost dutiful smile – which was equivalent to ignoring her. He went back to his book, one finger still slipped into their little brother's clenched fist. The boy, unlike her, hadn't been abandoned.

The sister's strategy wasn't working. She had to rid herself of the belief the firstborn might snap out of it if she simply said: "Please think of us, think of me." She was going to have to adapt, ready herself for the fight ahead, and learn the language of ceasefires and assaults.

The bus rides to school every morning were a form of ceasefire. The sister and the firstborn waited under a cement shelter at the side of a country road. When the bus slowed down, its brakes screeching, she was immediately relieved that each new kilometre would take them further away from the boy. She could then prattle on to her brother in the next seat, making up stories. He listened half-heartedly while staring out of the window, but at least she had him to herself. The most beautiful ceasefire had been the morning they'd gone to pick wild asparagus up in the mountains while the adults felled a cedar tree down in the valley. The parents had searched for them everywhere and they'd been punished. She hadn't cared as she knew he'd wanted to save her from that giant falling tree. It had been the same that evening in the courtyard when their father first explained that the boy was blind. Her elder brother had placed a hand on her shoulder. His protective instinct had been a certainty back then. It would never have occurred to her that it could disappear one day.

The assaults were the moments the firstborn spent without her: when he took the boy and laid him on the ground beside the river. She'd watch him go, stepping cautiously onto the grassy slope, the boy stuck to his chest. He always headed to the same spot. She knew he'd place him under the pine tree, near where the current was slowest, between the two waterfalls. That's where she'd end up barging in on them, shattering their peace. She'd splash around, stack pebbles into pyramids and catch pond skaters. She'd scream to exaggerate her happiness, claim her rightful place and remind them that she existed. Sometimes, the firstborn would reach for his camera and take a picture of them, the sister standing and the boy lying flat. Though he never took a picture just of her, ankle-deep in the water. She would stare unblinkingly at the camera to assert her presence.

But it was never enough.

For a while, in order not to lose the firstborn completely, she thought she had to love the boy the way he did. She, too, laid out the big cushions in the courtyard, but her clumsiness ended up betraying her. She once pulled a cushion so hard it tore and thousands of tiny white beads spilled onto the slate stones. The firstborn said nothing as she scooped them up, cursing to herself.

He simply added a cushion to the list of things to buy. The sister carried on with her attempts. She took an interest in vegetable purées; in administering the doses of the anti-seizure medication, Depakene; in noises, too – as the boy, of course, could only hear. She rustled leaves next to his ears, and did her utmost to describe what she saw around them. The words didn't come. She found the exercise ludicrous. She sighed impatiently and wanted to shake the boy, shout at him to sit up and stop fooling around. She wanted to tell him everyone was bored of his behaviour.

She did her best to follow his black eyes, too, as they roamed from one point to another. His blindness troubled her deeply. She didn't like his shifting gaze. Sometimes, her eyes would meet his on their sweep back and forth. For a split second she'd be overwhelmed by unease. Then the boy's eyes set off again on their slow path. And though she knew this gaze of his was incapable of seeing a thing, that it was defective, she couldn't help but read dark menace within it. It was as if it were saying: Beware of your feelings. I know I disgust you, but it's not my fault. We're of the same blood, you and me.

She put her cheek against his, right on the spot where, it was true, his skin felt the milkiest and softest. But very quickly she felt as if she were getting cramps; she recoiled at the smell of his mouth – the whiff of purée, of boiled vegetables. Then there was the stench of his nappy, which had to be changed, and she certainly wasn't going to get involved in that.

She called out to the firstborn. Whenever she saw him lean over the boy and speak in a voice so tender it became gooey – all the while grabbing the spread-out ankles to lift his bottom and slip a clean nappy underneath – she wished her elder brother would just turn around and suggest that they went and sat down by the river instead, no-one else but them.

Other times, she thought she might as well make the most of the unresponsive boy, and invent games for herself. So she fetched elastic hair ties, make-up, a lace collar and a headband. She sat cross-legged beside the rocker seat and drew red dots on the boy's cheeks, smearing black over his eyebrows and powdering his eyelids. Sometimes she braided his thick hair, too. He didn't seem surprised or put up any resistance. He only pulled a slight face when the brush scraped his cheek, or raised his eyebrows when an unknown material touched his head. The firstborn would then appear, with a grim look on his face, and remove the boy. He didn't scold his sister; he simply held his brother tight against his neck. The boy seemed to weigh no more than a feather in his arms. She had no idea how he did it.

*

She'd only carried the boy once. She'd gone over to the rocker chair in the sitting room, summoned up her courage, and stuck her hands under his armpits. But she'd forgotten about his floppy neck and as she'd lifted him up his head had flipped backwards and been left dangling. She'd let go in fear and the boy had fallen backwards, his head bouncing off the fabric of the chair, before slumping forward. The upper half of his body had tipped to one side and he'd become still, crying out in discomfort. It was the only time the firstborn had shown real anger – finding his brother like a disjointed puppet, his calves hanging limply, his head drooped. He didn't blame his sister. Instead he raged against everyone's indifference. Why had no-one noticed that the boy needed to be comfortable? Just because he was maladapted, it didn't mean he had to be left wonky and with his neck twisted. His parents calmed him. They understood why he was so upset, but everything was alright. The boy had stopped whimpering. What's more, they'd just bought some new tracksuit bottoms for him. Perhaps it was the perfect time to try them on? The parents didn't berate the sister.

Anger kept her upright. It gave her a valuable solidity. She needed it to remain standing. Those who lay down had no such strength. Anger granted her secret moments of revolt. She'd clench her fists in her pockets and punch her pillow repeatedly at bedtime in a vicious, consoling ritual. When a new storm blew in, and the wind roared like a great cat, and the mountains shivered with wicked delight, she felt at peace. She could lift her face towards the pewter-grey sky and suck in the tension blasting its way through the grass. It seemed to her that the river was grumbling with joy. She looked forward to the thunder and rain because she finally felt understood.

Since she frowned all the time and stayed stubbornly silent whenever she was asked a question, her parents sent her to see a psychologist. The practice was on the road into town; visitors had to leave their cars in the parking lot of a nearby industrial estate. At first, the sister felt harassed by the vastness of the place. Then, she relaxed. The flashing neon signs, the shops the size of warehouses and the whirring to-and-fro of cars calmed her in the way storms did. Excess soothed her. Unfortunately, the consulting room displayed no such extravagance or exuberance. Nothing in it appealed to her. Quite the opposite. She immediately hated the padded dullness of the room. She felt as if she were being held in some sort of incubator. The carpet, soft armchairs, the essential-oil diffuser and the pastoral scenes on the walls were an attack on her senses.

The psychologist was young. He had a silky voice and observant eyes. She answered all his questions with shrugs, so he gave her some paper and pencils. She wanted to tell him she was twelve years old and no longer at nursery school, but she thought better of it as her mother was waiting in the room next door. She began to draw.

She drew pictures for six months. After that, when she'd run out of inspiration, she coloured whole sheets in and pressed down as hard as she could on her pencils to make the lead snap.

The second psychologist lived in a village beyond town. It took an hour to get there each time. He nodded and smiled for three months, fully focused on her, while she ran through the various menus at her school canteen.

The third psychologist lived in a nearer village. He worked from a surgery which also housed a doctor, a dentist and a physiotherapist. The waiting room was basic, with nothing but plastic chairs in it. Every so often, the door would open and names would be called out. Then, people, often with splints on their limbs, stood up. The psychologist was a woman of indeterminate age with her hair in a messy bun. She wanted to talk to the mother. She had a few questions for her. Had she breastfed her children? Did she come home late from work? Did she love her husband? Did she love her own mother? Did she know that a "dysfunctional bond" could be transmitted from one generation to the next? Seeing her mother shrink into her chair like a bullied and browbeaten schoolgirl, the sister felt the same rage that kept her upright. Sometimes, she thought, daughters have to protect their mothers. The mother therefore didn't object when her daughter grabbed her by the hand and yanked her out of the room. The psychologist chased behind them, the pitter-patter of her feet like the trotting of a mule. "Oh come on, stop," she said as they headed for the exit. "Go and see a shrink yourself," the sister shouted back. Mother and daughter burst out laughing when they reached the car; the mother bent over the steering wheel, wiping her eyes. The sister wasn't sure if she was crying or laughing, so she hugged her. The two of them stayed like that, stuck to one another, in an embrace above the gearstick.

One day, the mother's friends came to visit from town. As usual, the boy was lying on the big cushions in the shaded part of the courtyard. There was a feeling of deep calm. We, the stones, ancient custodians that we are, can detect buried tensions, however. The mother had offered her friends something to drink. The women kept on glancing over at the boy. We sensed their unease. They finally made up their mind to question the mother. Was the boy quadriplegic? Was he in pain? Did he understand what was being said to him? Could his "illness" (that was the term they employed) have been predicted in any way? The mother put down the jug she was holding and replied. No, his spine wasn't severed, nor was there any specific injury. His brain simply didn't transmit the right signals. He didn't seem to feel pain, although he could express himself through tears and laughter. He could hear, too. So, he's blind, is he? Yes. Will he ever be able to speak or stand up on his own? No. So none of this was visible on the ultrasound? No. Did he contract a disease in the womb or was it something you were carrying? No. It's a genetic defect, a faulty chromosome, which can't be identified early or treated. It just appears at birth, randomly.

The sister listens to all this and she scorns her mother's attitude. She knows she isn't capable of such generosity. We can hear the turmoil, the wretched guilt inside her. She says to herself: I have no trace of my mother's sweet kindness in me. I have no use for simple words. My mother trusts others; she speaks openly, without fear. I don't know how. I don't share her rock-solid poise. I don't possess the grit of mountain women. I don't understand their centuries of fearless compliance. Women like my mother stand tall, despite their porcelain-like ankles. Their submission is an illusion: they are thought to be brittle like the rocks that surround them but, just like slate, they are solid precisely because they splinter. They are shrewd when faced with fate, and wise enough not to defy it. They bend and adapt. They prepare for future solace. They organise ways to resist. They bide their time and outsmart sorrow. It's no coincidence, the sister tells herself, that the firstborn values endurance above all else. He puts up with things rather than fighting them. I can't do that. I'm forever in conflict. I bump into life, scream my refusal of it. The battle is one-sided, and I'll lose for sure, but I persist in challenging. I refuse. I'm not like the mighty women of these mountains.

The sister stood and slipped through the medieval door to escape up the slopes. Her trainers slid on the rock face. She picked herself up each time and carried on, one shin soon streaked with blood. After the narrow *draille* track, she sat down in the bracken. In the distance she saw the three grey cherry tree trunks that had died at the same time as the farmer. Their skeletons rose out of the grass. Everything around her was in perfect balance. The summer rain had left a slick of varnish on the stones. An aroma of water-gorged soil and fresh roots swept over her. The roots were in tune with the trees, the ponds, the leaves, the faraway sound of sheep bells. The self-sustaining harmony of it all felt intolerable and prompted in her a powerful feeling of unfairness. Nature, just like the boy, was cruelly indifferent. Its beauty was heartless.

It heard nothing, not even the distress of a girl like her. She knew it would carry on thriving long after she was gone. Nature didn't seek forgiveness for the cruelty of its laws. She bent down and picked up a stone. She set about destroying a holm oak sapling beside her. The branches were supple and more than once they whipped back and hit her in the face – as if the tree were defending itself. Her arms were soon covered in scratches as she was wearing only a vest. She carried on attacking the sapling with the stone until it had been pummelled into a carpet of branches and leaves. Drops of sweat stung her eyes.

On the way back home, she came across a stray dog lying under the porch opposite the woodshed. The animal's position made it look strange. It was sleeping with its head askew, as if its legs were detached from its body and cast aside. The dog had been overwhelmed by the heat, and was probably healthy enough, but the sight of it transfixed the girl. It seemed to her that the boy's oddness was becoming contagious. Every creature around her was dislocating. Soon, the whole world would weaken and turn inside out. She, too, would wake with a feeble neck and heavy knees. Seized by panic, she ran down to the orchard by the river. She tripped over some fallen apples. She got up again. She stepped into the water. Her trainers prevented her from slipping. She kept going further into the shade. The surface of the river was black and scarcely disturbed by the skating of water insects. It felt like thousands of needles were pricking her calves and thighs, her hips too, despite the shorts she was wearing. The river washed the wounds on her shin, the scratches on her arms. Her vest had become drenched in sweat, her clammy skin covered in a thin film of dirt. Her chest was rising and falling too fast. She was shivering with cold or sadness, she didn't know which. A question was opening a chasm inside her; its few words battered her: "Who will help me?" The river weighed her down and stopped her from falling headfirst into that chasm. She opened her arms, lifted her fingers out of the water to scramble its smooth surface, and stayed in that position, limbs straight and quivering. Had anyone come across her at that point they would have taken fright. The young girl was waist-deep in the river, clothed, her hair dishevelled, her body stretched out in the shape of a cross, gasping for breath. She tried to calm herself by closing her eyes and focusing on the noises around her – not realising she was behaving like the boy. The stillness of the afternoon swept over her. The chirping of birds reached her and with it the rumble of waterfalls. She could sense the vastness of the surrounding mountains scorched by summer sun. Only the insects continued to hum, darting in and out of the broiled, static plants. A dragonfly skimmed her ear. Soon everything began to fall back into place. The mountains had waited for the crisis to blow over. They had done this for millennia, standing by until human anger subsided. She felt like a small moody child. She opened her eyes and looked up. The alder branches were weaving a roof above her head.

The only person who lightened her heart was her grandmother. She'd once lived in the hamlet, but had since retired to the city. She said she was "made for city living". She wore bright red lipstick and low heels and kept her dark hair in a convoluted bun. She never took her bracelets off and insisted on sleeping in a light kimono even during the winter months. She invariably wore a silk dress at Christmas events. No-one was fooled by any of this, however. She was still a woman of the Cévennes through and through. Mainly because, without being aware of it, she liked to repeat the local mantra of "loyalty, endurance and decency", a magic formula that seemed to solve all problems. Also because she'd been in the Resistance during the war, a period she never discussed apart from once, when she showed her granddaughter a tunnel dug into one of the pillars of the stone bridge. To reach it, you had to go down into the orchard, head up the river and stand beneath the bridge. There, in the thick expanse of stone, was a stretch of darkness, a tunnel that had sheltered persecuted families. They would clamber inside from the riverbank. The elders had to be lifted up. Everyone crawled in on their elbows, as if into a deep, black mouth. The children always went first.

The grandmother clearly belonged to the Cévennes, too, because she could tell a medlar from a plum tree at a glance. She'd also, to the amazement of everyone in the valley, managed to plant a row of bamboo trees at the end of the orchard. And she could cook with whatever wild plants she found. When she saw a twisted trunk she'd say: "That's an unhappy tree." She knew, too, where the wind took root. She could identify the exact spot where it had sprung up. She'd say: "It's coming from the west. It's the fiendish Rouergue from the Aveyron, cloying and gluey. It'll give you a chest infection. Remember it'll turn to drizzle after lunch, around coffee-time." And, indeed, it then did rain at that time. Her ear was so attuned she could not only recognise the twittering of a wagtail, but she could also tell its age. She's a witch dressed as a duchess, the sister thought.

During the holidays, the grandmother moved into the first house in the hamlet. The children only had to cross the courtyard and walk along the road for a short while in order to visit her. She lived alone, but near the family nevertheless. It was the way hamlets had operated in the old days. Her terrace was bordered by a wooden balustrade which looked out onto the river. Beyond it, rising steeply into the sky, were the mountains, mahogany in colour. If you stretched your hand out you almost felt able to touch them. The sound of water, strangled into a narrow gully between the mountainside and the base of the terrace wall, grew until it burst into the fullness of a booming echo. The sister loved this place. It seemed to be scraped from the rock face itself, caught in crashing foam. She preferred the terrace to the courtyard, the enclosed area where the boy lay on his cushions.

It was on the terrace, where she sat in a wicker chair, that her grandmother slipped a wooden yo-yo into her hand and said: "I gave ones like these to the children who hid under the bridge. There are always downs in life, but ups too." When she was with her grandmother, there was no stolen brother and no brother who stole.

The grandmother and sister would lock themselves away all afternoon to make orange-flavoured waffles (a Portuguese recipe the grandmother loved), as well as onion fritters and elderflower jam. Their faces enveloped in steam, they'd also skin recently boiled, piping-hot chestnuts, and crumble them into a copper bowl, releasing a smell of vanilla-scented sugar. They'd sell the jams they produced at the market and treat themselves to what the grandmother called "little manicures". She often described her childhood in the local silkworm farms, the vast houses they called *"magnaneries"*, which were without inner doors or walls. It had been hot inside these buildings filled with leaves and silkworms. They had to wait for the precise moment the silkworms began spinning their cocoons. "Those cocoons were the bane of my life," she said. "We had to unpick them carefully and boil the silkworms before they had a chance to become butterflies." The astonished sister tried to imagine the sound of thousands of caterpillars munching thousands of mulberry leaves. "Don't bother," the grandmother said. "Modern life takes those kind of sounds with it."

Sometimes the grandmother would drive the sister up into the mountains to look at a special tree. It was a cedar that had grown on top of a rock overhanging the road. In theory it was impossible. No tree could push its roots deep into stone. And yet this plant stretched up and out with all the grace of a swan's neck. The grandmother liked to stop the car, bend over the steering wheel and examine the tree's thin trunk. "That one wants to live," she'd say. "Like you."

Then she drove on so they could admire a spectacular landscape: a valley narrowing between two mountains, the sparkle of a single thread signalling the presence of a river. You could see their village, too, nestled in the folds, like a baby pressed against its mother's bosom. The grandmother wasn't looking down, however, but up at another village, the one where she'd been born – a nearly inaccessible cluster of dark stones balanced on the rim of a cliff.

"It grew on the edge of the abyss," she said.

Just like me, the sister thought.

They drove home in silence, the sister dangling one arm out of the lowered window. Her grandmother remained fully concentrated on the road. Only the rasp of the engine could be heard, faltering before each hairpin bend and then catching its breath on the downward slope. As the village came into view, beyond a curve in the road, the grandmother suddenly rolled out a list of questions, without taking her eyes off the road:

"Which tree has a cone studded with little snake tongues?"

"The Douglas pine," the sister said, still staring out of the window.

"If you found a log from a young ash tree, what would the bark feel like?"

"Smooth and grey."

"What leaves are fan-shaped and without a central ridge?"

"Ginkgo biloba leaves."

"The bark of which tree can be peeled to treat eczema?"

"Beech."

"No."

"Oak."

"Yes."

The grandmother didn't speak much. Like many people of few words she communicated through actions instead. She brought the right kind of Walkman back from the city, and the latest trendy trainers. She subscribed her granddaughter to magazines for girls her age and took her to see new films in town – because of that, the sister could say "I've seen *Romancing the Stone*" in the play-ground. She could also have a heated discussion on Modern Talking's style of music, wear a Chevignon sweatshirt and chew gum. The grandmother had allowed her to participate in the world. She'd provided a sense of normality. Much later, when she was an adult, the sister was heard saying to a friend: "When a child isn't well, you need to keep an eye out for any siblings." Then she added, but more for herself: "The ones who are in good health don't make a fuss. They adapt to the jagged-ness of life, to its sorrow, without asking for anything in return. They're like lighthouse keepers who fear the rising sea, yet they can't refuse their duty. They stand like watchmen in the night, muddling through as best they can, trying not to be cold or frightened, but it's not possible never to be cold or frightened. You need to look out for such children."

The sister didn't feel angry when she was with her grandmother. This didn't stop the latter from watching over her even more as she'd understood the firstborn's attachment to the boy and the parents' sadness. She helped them by making a compote of Pippin apples or quinces. She carried it from her house every day, along the road, crossing the courtyard, and left it on the kitchen table in a bowl, for the "little one". She also took the boy to the day nursery when the mother couldn't and picked him up if no-one else had time. Her bracelets chimed whenever she held him in her arms, clumsily but firmly. He looked all twisted but didn't moan. She didn't speak much to the boy. That was the way she was. Sometimes, she left a pair of new slippers next to the bowl of compote, or a pack of cottonwool pads and vials of saline solution. How did she know the parents were running low? No-one could tell. The grandmother just knew. The sister wasn't jealous of this. On the contrary, her grandmother's attentiveness to the boy's needs eased the weight of her guilt.

*

As the months passed, the sister wiped the boy from her life and opted for wilful blindness instead. She ignored her parents' crumpled faces when they returned home from another day filled with administrative tasks of all kinds. She chose not to see; offered no support. She displayed no emotion when the parents announced that the boy would have to be taken to a specialised care home run by nuns, a place tucked away in a meadow, hundreds of kilometres from them. She could imagine the turmoil in the firstborn's heart whenever she sat next to him, but she chose to stare into her plate and carefully pick the tomatoes out of her salad instead. That evening she asked if she could call her grandmother, as her friend, Noémie, had said that François Mitterand was more handsome than Kevin Costner. The matter had to be discussed urgently.

When the boy left for the care home in the meadow, she was able to breathe again. The awkward feelings of disgust, anger and shame went with him. It was as if he'd taken the dark side of her soul away. She'd no longer feel pain, she thought. She even dared to hope that her elder brother would return to her. Yet he seemed to have evaporated. That's the only word she could find to describe the way the firstborn's body erased itself, how his footsteps left an imprint of unfathomable sadness. He was pale and his stare was empty. He had no strength in him. He'd become like the boy.

She had to seek life elsewhere. She made new friends and got invited to birthday parties and sleepovers, although she never organised a single event at her house. She took part in sporting events, commented on the gossip in *OK! Magazine* and exchanged messages with her grandmother to make sure everything was ready for her next return home to the hamlet. She liked to inspect the cold house before her grandmother arrived, lay the fire, make the bed, check the hot-water storage tank was on and hose down the terrace. Once the grandmother had settled back into the house, the sister didn't trouble her for hugs or kisses. She preferred to almost move into the house instead. The girl knew every corner of the place: the chipped rims on the mugs, the sound of the tap dripping in the sink, the smell of vanilla sugar and soap in the kitchen. The grandmother had refurbished the main room and designed an open-plan kitchen. She believed this to be the epitome of modern living, having all too often seen her mother cooking while shut away on her own. The white kitchen, with its light-coloured wood surfaces, stretched down the wall of the main room which also contained a fireplace and a sitting area. The grandmother invited friends over all the time. The sister drank coffee with women called Marthe, Rose and Jeanine who sat lined up on the sofa like the shiny pearls of an antique necklace. They put their teacups down with great care and left whole swathes of their sentences unfinished. This wasn't down to old age, as the sister had thought at first. It was because the women had already understood each other and felt no need to carry on talking. It led to intriguing, otherworldly conversations. Fragments of stories took shape, peppered with mysterious gaps: "the hollow bridge where the Schenkel family …"; "I planted it that day when the irrigation canal …"; "wait, wasn't he the one who promised …"; "when my hands were burning from the cocoons …". After that, they alluded to summertime feasts, moments of fear, wayward boyfriends. The women often chuckled, without the sister understanding why. Theirs were throaty laughs, almost rough in sound, which didn't match the women's well-groomed appearances. The patchy conversations then resumed: "The Mignargue dance was the best …"; "they searched for his finger everywhere, found it stuck … with the wedding ring still on it …"; "a German face, stiff as a rake". They nodded, smiled, and punctuated the pauses in their conversation with sighs and exclamations. The powerful emotions the women shared, rather than language itself, formed the basis of their communication.

*

The sister forgot about the boy and her elder brother when she was with these women. She felt ageless and tried to piece together stories from the scraps she'd heard. When evening came, her mother often poked her head round the sitting-room door, greeting Marthe, Rose or Jeanine, and said: "It's late, *Maman*. Can I have my daughter back? I'm serving dinner."

The sister would grudgingly stand up to leave. The idea of sitting down to eat at the same table as the first-born crushed her. She was learning to flee him as to get close to him again meant stoking up too much unhappiness, laying bare the pain of having been separated from him. In fact, to get close to him meant destroying the courage she'd built up; it was like lying down and dying, dying of injustice, of what the boy had inflicted on them by turning everything upside down.

She'd decided to speak less and less to her elder brother.

She made sure to bump into him, though, when she came out of the bathroom with her hair still wet. And she spotted him through the window of his school bus while she waited for her own to arrive (she loved seeing his profile as he sat at the front, eyes straight ahead). There were times too when she happened upon his glasses at the end of the kitchen table or noticed him standing in the orchard. She didn't know why he was there, but she suspected that he was stirring up memories of the boy. He'd probably once placed the rocker chair in that exact spot. A time without her; a time which didn't belong to her.

She accepted all this because accepting was not as painful as feeling excluded. She preferred an elder brother who was lost in sorrow than one who was happy without her; an elder brother who perhaps didn't laugh anymore, but who didn't turn away from her either. She'd lost him. But at least she'd been given his ghost in return.

This state of affairs had been achieved without tears and it persisted for several months. The parents went and fetched the boy for the holidays. The sister avoided getting close to him. She was too busy at her grandmother's house or out with friends to whom she hid the existence of this sibling. Hearing her speak, one would have thought she only had an elder brother and that she couldn't invite anyone back because the house was being renovated.

The sister didn't work that hard at school. The teachers complained about her rowdiness. They said they were worried: she's barely fifteen, and she already has so much anger. When the teacher in her class asked the pupils to comment on a Nietzsche quote – "That which does not kill us makes us stronger" – she yelled: "That's not true, that which does not kill us makes us weaker. Whoever said that doesn't understand a thing about life. They just want to blame themselves and glorify pain." She said this so scathingly, as if it were a declaration of war, and with such rage, that the parents were summoned to the school. But the fury simmering away inside her was only getting louder and louder, and she wanted revenge. If she was going to live surrounded by ruins, she thought, she might as well lay waste to the world around her. When she came back from the hairdresser's with her head half shaved, her grandmother was the only one to find the haircut interesting. Her parents greeted her new appearance with utter weariness. The firstborn didn't appear to notice.

She didn't care about the courtyard, the wall, or us, the stones. She crossed our area without stopping. She went determinedly on her way, more wound up than ever. If she'd bothered to notice us, it surely would only have been to pry one of us from the wall to strike someone. We'd witnessed this ill wind before; we knew all too well how it electrifies the body. Enough violence had taken place in that courtyard over the years. It was radiating from that girl: a thirst for committing the irreparable, for reaching a point of no return. She dreamed of destruction and letting out screams that would never be heard. By June, she was hovering around village dances, her eyelashes thick with black mascara, looking for trouble. The dances were small gatherings, held in squares, next to tennis courts, youth centres and campsites, where the ground was flat and wide enough to set up a sound system, a stage and a bar. The sister drank sangria – a lot of sangria – from plastic cups and spoke loudly. The paper lanterns made her want to set fire to things. She sat with her friends and watched as groups from different valleys arrived on their mopeds. At these gatherings, before asking someone their name, you'd say: "Where do you come from?" And they'd reply, "From Valbonne," or "Montdardier." The sister admired the certainty of these answers each time. Of course, she, too, came from a specific hamlet, in a specific valley, but she wouldn't have known what to say. She felt landless; she had no answers left inside her. Instead, she provoked; showed her spitefulness. She was itching for a fight. She soon got into one round the back of a row of loudspeakers which served to drown out her screams. An infuriated, drunken boy knocked her to the ground. Her mouth filled with sand and gravel, a taste she'd forever associate with the sound of Cyndi Lauper's "I Drove All Night" as it was being blasted across the dance floor at that very moment. She lost a tooth, staggered from behind the stage and its vibrating speakers, and walked away, one hand across her mouth. Her father came to fetch her in the car. He always came and got her. Often, he'd find her throwing up, her face smudged with black-tainted tears. This time, he gritted his teeth, handed her a pack of tissues and drove her home.

She went to upper secondary school. She got into fights there, too, during breaks between classes, and in the canteen. After tipping her desk upside down when a teacher told her off, she was asked to leave. Her parents couldn't find another school willing to take her in the middle of the academic year. The only place available and willing to have her was expensive and far away. They enrolled her nonetheless. They had to leave early each morning at the same time the mother went to work. In the back of the car, above the boy's specially designed seat, hung a mobile with a smiling teddy and two bunches of bells. They chimed whenever the car swerved. The sister loathed the noise.

Unexpectedly, the boy had to return home one morning. He'd developed a fever. The nuns didn't want his illness to spread. The parents had to look after him until the fever cleared. The mother took a few days off work and the boy had to accompany them to school. The sister sank into the back seat and avoided looking his way. She heard him sigh happily when the mother turned the radio on and music filled the enclosed space.

But at some point on the road, he began to whimper. His padded anorak was squeezing him too tightly into the car seat. The mother parked on the hard shoulder, undid her seatbelt, and got out to open the rear door. The hugeness of the dawn sky, a smell of dew and damp tarmac, and the squawking of birds burst into the car. The dark mountains were silhouetted against the pink horizon. The sister had always preferred the night. She heard her mother whisper to the boy and undo his seat straps. In order to loosen them further, she had to remove him from the car seat, but she had nowhere to put him down. He was heavy and slipped about easily as she could only hold him with one hand under his bottom while her other hand fiddled with the straps. The sister didn't offer to help. She sat stubbornly still and stared straight ahead at the mountain tops ringed with purple mist. The mother ended up having to walk round the car to open the door on the other side and lay the boy down, and then walk back again to adjust the straps. She didn't request anything of her daughter. When she eventually sat back behind the steering wheel, her forehead dripping with sweat, she turned the radio to full volume.

*

The sister signed up to boxing lessons. She had to cycle along a country lane to get there. The road was dangerous and she liked that. Attentive to her needs, the grandmother bought her the right boxing gear. With her face half hidden by a helmet and her thighs in a shiny pair of shorts, the sister rehearsed hooks, jabs, ducking and weaving, shuffles and slides on the terrace (inadvertently smashing the boy's bowl of compote in the process). She shouted as she boxed, straining her voice to be heard over the rush of the river until she was worn out. The grandmother applauded from her wicker chair as if she were at the opera.

At least once a week, the two of them sat in front of the fire and read a book about Portugal, the country where the grandmother had travelled for her one and only trip abroad. It had been her honeymoon. She spoke about the trip constantly and invariably ended up bringing out an old photographic book which opened with a map. She'd point her painted fingernail at the southern tip of the country and say "Carrapateira" in a soft voice. It was there, in a white village hanging on the edge of the Atlantic, that their bus had broken down. She reminisced about the ocean's roar, and a wind so brutal that the trees grew at a slant, their trunks bowed in submission. There had been low houses, too, with octopuses hung out to dry on nails in their walls. She'd brought back recipes and used them over the next fifty years to make pastries like the orange-scented waffles the sister loved. The girl adored the word "Carrapateira", and dreamed of tattooing it on her skin. It sounded prettier than "Rifamycin".

One afternoon, as Marthe, Rose and Jeanine were sipping tea, it became very clear to the sister that these women were inhabited by a kind of peace. The realisation was a little like the surprise she and the firstborn used to get when, in the days when they did everything together, they came across the crayfish they'd been endlessly searching for: a bleary, small black body crawling over the pebbles, at the bottom of the water. It would elicit a shudder of wonder in both of them. The grandmother served tea to her friends with blue-painted eyelids and fragmented conversation. The women didn't seem at all surprised by the presence of a teenager with a half-shaved head and eyes darkened by make-up the colour of coal. The sister understood how different she was to these old ladies. She felt she had lost their mix of meekness and acceptance. She lived in a separate world where vegetation and vegetative states mingled, a blurring of trees and children laid flat on cushions. Her life was limited to that. It seemed to her that she was much older than her grandmother. She jumped up, barely startling the old ladies with her sudden movement, turned the volume up on her Walkman and set off. She wanted to stamp around the mountainside to the rhythm of "I Drove All Night" by Cyndi Lauper.

The sister got up early at weekends. She was used to leaving the house at dawn. The tiled floor felt cold as she walked past the boy's empty room and then her elder brother's bedroom packed with things. She put on her long jacket and went outside. Her face was immediately shrouded in fresh air. The earth exhaled spirals of musty white fumes. She seemed sure that her memory had taken the same form as the earth; it, too, secreted wisps of a mist that never fully lifted. The only suggestion of wakefulness was the river, locked into its never-ending cycle of hurtling water. The mountains reached into the air above her, their backs arched, their bases seemingly fastened to the thread of a road. On the bridge, in her jumper, arms crossed, she sniffed at the air and felt the full force of her pain: she and her elder brother no longer shared anything. He would have loved these mornings. She wondered how one should mourn a living person. Her rage against the boy returned. He'd wrecked every-thing. A pang of pity hit her, and then she was filled with revulsion at an image of his open mouth, his breath, his whimpers of discomfort and contentment. After that, she felt the despondency which crushed her each time. It made all the questions that swirled around in her head seem pointless. She dabbed her eyes.

"Why do your friends, Marthe, Rose and Jeanine, not judge me?"

"Because they're sad, and when you're sad, you don't judge others."

"That's not true. I know loads of people who are sad and they're still mean."

"Then those people are unhappy, not sad."

"…"

"Have some more waffles."

The grandmother's life went the way of all forebears. Dressed in her light kimono, she collapsed one morning in her kitchen, around breakfast time, chestnut and vanilla smells wafting around her. She was found later that day. One of her friends, Marthe, Rose or Jeanine, had popped by. Looking through the glass panes of the front door, they spotted a hand with red-painted nails flat against the floor, in a heap of white sugar and the shards of a broken china bowl.

The fire brigade didn't bother staying long. She'd been dead for hours, they told the parents.

It was the end of the world for the sister. It was exactly

how her elder brother had felt when the boy left for the care home in the meadow.

Her mother told her on the way back from school, gripping the steering wheel and staring ahead, fearful of her daughter's reaction.

"Your grandmother died this morning."

The sister repeated what her heart was telling her: "No."

Her mother thought she'd misheard. "What do you mean, 'no'?"

"No."

A breakdown can take its opposite form. Despair sometimes becomes a form of hardness. This is exactly what happened. The sister's desire to strike out, that impulse of hers, the boiling anger – all those forces that drummed away inside her disappeared to give way to frozen nothingness. Her heart shrank under a layer of coldness. Her new toughness came quite naturally to her. She simply turned to stone. Her feelings had been wrenched from her. She no longer had any. All that was over.

Even her way of walking changed. We noticed straightaway that her steps no longer seemed hurried or unsteady. Instead, she seemed to be marching. She had a discipline to her, feet firmly on the ground, knees stiff, head held high. She opened the medieval door onto the courtyard with a new and slow precision. Her manner of flicking her hair away from her face lost its impatience. Her hand now seemed to obey some meticulous plan as she seized the strands and tucked them behind her ear. There was a resoluteness to her gestures. All doubt and emotion had been banished.

We realised that this metamorphosis was complete the night the father lost control for the first time. The strain of life had finally worn his patience thin. Since the boy's birth, he'd done his best to guide the household forward. From time to time, though, we'd noted the way he silently stared at his son before going to fetch his woolly hat. For the most part, however, he joked and tried to stay positive. One Christmas Eve, seeing a single, small wrapped gift next to the boy's slippers, he'd said: "You have to admit the great thing about a disabled child is that they're a lot cheaper at this time of year." Even the mother had giggled.

Yet the sister had noticed how her father preferred the axe to the chainsaw when cutting wood. More than once, she'd found him in front of the woodshed in a sweat, shaking with the sort of viciousness she recognised in herself. He raised his arms up high before bringing the axe down, putting his full weight behind it. The action ended with a terrible grunt, half-hiccup, half-sob, a noise she'd never heard him emit before. The wood smashed into pieces and ripped through the air like blades. Her father had a wiry body like most men in the Cévennes. At that moment, though, she felt as if he were a giant creature made of raw muscle. He yanked the axe out the wood and raised it high again, wrists shaking.

She'd seen him battle the vast coils of brambles along the river. There again he'd chosen not to use an electric trimmer but a pair of shears, which he opened and closed with frightening speed as if he needed to obliterate the undergrowth. His eyes stared blankly and his jaw stayed clenched, the same as when he drove her home from village dances.

Come evening, the father returned to his old self and treated the family to an onion tart and wild boar stew – "You need to be resourceful in this part of the world," he joked. He then spoke about the redevelopment of a co-operative and the old silk factory that was being turned into a museum. Each time, an ill-defined uneasiness took hold of the sister, a feeling of danger that made her want to hurl her plate against the wall.

She wasn't surprised, therefore, when one evening her father – with the same grunting fury he displayed when chopping wood – grabbed a hiker by the scruff of the neck and shoved him back onto the road when he insisted on leaving his camper van by the disused mill. The savagery of the incident spurred the sister into action. She took stock of the situation: their father's dangerous outburst had barely registered with her brother; her mother was too crushed by her own mother's death to notice – in fact, she had barely spoken since the grandmother had died. So, while the hiker limped off, threatening retaliation, the sister contemplated the wasteland around her. She pictured herself whispering to the boy, her lips pressed against his pale cheek – "You're the disaster" – before chasing the thought away. There was no point piling chaos on chaos. They had to move beyond sorrow. She needed to rescue the family from danger. Her father was becoming violent, her mother mute, and her elder brother had already become a ghost. She would fight back. A new strength, razor-sharp and icy, took hold of her. It was the sort of strength that stems from dealing with emergencies, which she'd understood from witnessing how the sky could pummel the mountains, uproot trees, flip cars, sweep lives away, and how people reacted in such circumstances: they staked the trees with ropes, raised the dams so the water could surge forward unhampered, and built buttresses. So that was it. She'd build buttresses to strengthen her family.

She needed a strategy. She found a notepad and listed the issues, as well as the solutions required.

Issue 1: Her elder brother felt better whenever he was

with the boy. The solution was, therefore, to bring the boy back from the care home in the meadow more often. She noted the exact dates of his returns in the notepad so that she could make sure to fill the fridge, heat his room and prepare pots of yoghurt as there were no fruit compotes anymore. It wasn't out of affection for the boy, but to help her elder brother. This was a military-like family recovery plan. Efficiency had to prevail.

Issue 2: Her elder brother was cutting himself off from others. The solution was to keep an eye on him and monitor how much time he spent alone. When he went over the limit she'd set, she'd disturb him with the excuse of needing help with her maths homework (without revealing she'd already solved the problem).

Issue 3: The firstborn was no longer fulfilling his duties as elder brother. No-one cared about the assigned order anymore, as everything had been blown to pieces. She now had to reverse their roles and protect him.

Issue 4: It would cheer her parents to know she'd become a good student, and it would be one less thing for them to worry about. She began to study hard. Her task: to crush her peers and become top of her class. She drew no satisfaction from this at all, apart from knowing that she was relieving the pressure on her parents and ticking one more item off her list.

She acted methodically, like a soldier going into battle.

We watched her in the courtyard, pulling a chair up with one swift movement, throwing the notepad down as if she were slapping the garden table, charting progress with her pen. She was adapting to the situation, right before us, as her brother, her parents and countless others had done before her, winning our admiration. Perhaps, one day, the agility that's acquired when life kicks you around will come to be valued as a skill – one which enables you to regain balance on the tightrope of existence despite the torment.

The sister got rid of all things superfluous to her battle. She tidied her make-up away; forgot about going to the hairdresser. Saving her family required staying on track. She had no choice. She learned to appear detached even though she was choking up inside; to seem unconcerned at family meals; to say nothing in the playground. She imposed an ironclad discipline on herself. Her tight schedule kept her going. She did the shopping, prepared meals and hung the washing out by the mill. By sparing her mother the bother of these tasks, she gained an extra ten minutes with her to chat, sometimes even an hour. It got her talking once more. The sister scribbled subjects of conversation in her notepad, learning them off by heart to use at mealtimes. She found stories in the news-paper and had a particular interest in local events. She observed how her family reacted when she wove these stories into their discussions: parasite infestations in the vineyards; the Schengen Agreement; Bruce Springsteen's tour dates in the region; the TV crime series *"Les Cordier, juge et flic"* that her father watched; the heatwave they were predicting for June; the building of a new tourist office on the edge of town … She underlined the subjects which surprised her mother the most, the ones which elicited a comment from her father, and those which caught her elder brother's attention. She stopped spending time with her friends. She came straight home after school and turned down all invitations.

At first, her friends were riled by her unwillingness to join in. They circled round her with noisy, revving motorbikes in front of the school gates. Her bag was stolen, which led to a showdown. Her boxing lessons came in handy. Her tormentor ended up with a broken nose. The parents had to visit the wounded girl's family several times to make all sorts of amends.

After that, finally, the sister was left in peace. Despite being sociable, she ended up alone – just as she was alone in her mission to stop her family from drowning. If someone had told her at that point that a beautiful love awaited her in the future – one that would burst through the barriers she'd built up inside her and make her cherish life again – she would have laughed. But that's what would happen. The sister was to find someone who'd teach her how to let go. Back then, though, she knew nothing of such miracles.

Occasionally, she picked up her grandmother's yo-yo, but she quickly put it down again. No weakness could be tolerated. She never went back to her grandmother's house after the funeral and refused the light kimono they wanted to give her. She forgot the taste of orange waffles. She no longer went to boxing lessons or read the magazines her grandmother had subscribed her to. She became someone who never read or shared anything. She had no memory or connection to others. She had swapped the future for a goal. Like a commander, she had her eyes set on the horizon, her fists clenched. She had to stand firm without delay.

Months went by. Like a workhorse, the sister focused solely on results. She acted with speed, using as few words as possible, impervious to moods and feelings. She lost her last girlfriends. She had no regrets. She was pretty, yet she ignored all interest in her; she avoided social gatherings and was frosty with anyone who tried to get close. Only tangible outcomes motivated her. Had her elder brother smiled more than twice that day? Had her father stopped chopping wood like a madman?

What had her mother said that week? What glances had she exchanged with her father over dinner? Had talking about the local elections triggered a response? How high would her grades be by the end of the school term? She tracked renewal in all its forms. The world had become a statistical report in her notebook. On the left: the issues being steadily addressed. On the right: the subjects of conversation that were to be introduced the following day. She often fell asleep with the notebook open on her pillow.

The firstborn, meanwhile, was heading in the opposite direction. He was softening, opening up a little bit more each day. Whenever it was the holidays again, he became just as close to the boy as before. The sister, who no longer thought in terms of hope, but in terms of targets, was pleased. The firstborn had relaxed. There was a newfound steadiness to him. He was smiling. It didn't matter that it was because of the boy. He even complimented her on her hair, which had grown long again, and on her lack of make-up. She was relieved to think that she could cross another thing off her list.

She made the most of these more favourable circumstances to take the firstborn to the cinema. Without telling him, she avoided the row where she used to sit with her grandmother – always on the end of the aisle, "In case we have to run out." They spoke a bit about the blackberries which were enormous that year, and the petrol station attendant who'd run off with the village hairdresser. Then they brought up a few school memories. It was still all a bit tentative.

The film was soppy and badly dubbed. She didn't care. In the semi-darkness of the cinema, swathed in shifting and coloured shadows, she understood that the firstborn wouldn't ever be cured of the boy. A cure implied that he'd give up on suffering one day. But suffering was precisely what the boy had rooted deep inside him. It was his mark. So to be cured meant losing the boy, and the mark he'd left, for ever. She now knew that bonds with others came in endless guises. Conflict was a bond. As was suffering.

One evening, she asked the firstborn to take her home from school on his moped. The night sky was coloured an autumnal red. Days beforehand, a terrible storm, carried by a frenzied wind – the violence of which the grandmother would surely have predicted – had crashed down on the Cévennes. The water level had risen several metres, taking trees and cars with it. Two people had gone missing. The campsite overlooking the riverbank had been washed away; the terraces, wood stacks, greenhouses and onion crops, too. The glass in the shopfronts along the river had been blown out. The chemist described how her syringes floated off, and the butcher said he didn't have a single machine left operational. Luckily, the shopkeepers said, they'd been able to hurl themselves up the staircases to their first-floor flats or out of their back doors when the water had swept in.

Now the sister and the firstborn were witnessing the aftermath as night fell. Trees remained flattened, their branches coated in silt. Their dangling roots appeared almost obscene. The riverbed had widened by several metres. It was as if a pair of hands had appeared from the sky and wrenched the newly levelled banks apart. They had been stripped of their rocks and trees to become nothing more than broad stretches of sand. Sitting on the scooter luggage rack, the sister felt as if she were ploughing through a movable mass of stinking wet earth as it echoed with haunting sounds: the calls of prehistoric animals, the crackle of shadows, the wail of primeval woodland. The sister made sure not to squeeze her elder brother's waist too tightly as he drove carefully ahead. They didn't speak. She was left wondering whether she'd lost him for ever. But who decided such things? What could she do about it? Loss was part of her story now. They drove under a bridge destroyed by the storm. A section of the parapet had been carried away and a half-empty archway hung mid-air. It looked as though an ogre had bitten into the bridge and forgotten the last curved mouthful. An idea germinated in her mind the moment they passed the bridge: she was going to leave one day and seek a life elsewhere.

When the boy came home the following holidays, it was obvious he'd grown again. His constantly supine position had given him an even more enlarged palate so his messy teeth now stuck out further and his gums were swollen. There was no hiding his disability now. To her surprise, though, the sister didn't feel any disgust. She spent the summer both avoiding the boy and watching the first-born reconnect with him. She felt neither fear nor desire. She no longer tried to muscle in. At dinner, the subjects of conversation flowed as the firstborn commented on an item in the news or got his father onto the subject of his onion harvest. She'd then study the firstborn closely. His resemblance to the boy was as striking as before. He was the older version.

After a brief stint away from home, the firstborn swept into the sitting room one morning, leaving a smell of coffee in his wake. Dropping his rucksack, he rushed upstairs to the boy's bedroom and locked himself inside. The sister pictured him bent over the bed with the spirals, waiting for the boy to wake. The firstborn seemed happy to be home. She could tick that target off her list. Once again, he took to washing the boy, settling him under the pine tree by the river. The sister watched them from afar, like a general surveying the battlefield. What towel was the firstborn using for his snooze? How many times had he sat up to stroke the boy's cheek? Had he thought to take a bottle of water? Had he made sure there wasn't a hornets' nest in the tree trunk? Everything seemed in order. The firstborn was fine. She opened her notepad and scrubbed an item from her list. She was getting close to fulfilling her goal: her family was on the mend. It occurred to her then that she'd achieved such a level of hard-heartedness that she'd never be able to express her feelings again.

The boy's funeral proved her wrong.

Walking up the mountainside towards the grave, escorted by a small crowd of silent mourners, the sister felt steadily more petrified – and cold. A real coldness. It took over her whole body, numbing her limbs. Her chest felt constricted. She remembered how her elder brother had always wrapped the boy up warm. Now it was her turn to need a blanket around her. She was falling prey to the same chill. She panicked, wriggled her fingers and banged her feet to get the blood flowing. The iciness was turning to a slow bite. It almost burned, unlike the shock she got when she jumped in the river.

The sister walked with her eyes fixed on us, the stones,

in order to hide her agitation. We would have wanted to console her in some way. But who listens to us? No-one understands the paradox of how stones soften human-kind. We are used for shelter, as benches, as weapons and paths. We accompanied this girl, her head hanging low. She walked fast, jerkily, her body quivering, the loose rocks crunching under her feet like sand.

Once in the splendour of the woodland clearing, in its fairytale-like setting, the sister saw the oak branches stretched and bowed so close to the ground that they stirred the grass; and then her parents' legs, close enough together to look like they belonged to the same body; and the spiked railings around the small cemetery, some so sharp one had to think they'd been used to pierce hearts. The weight of the past few years fell on her at once, unfurling in a rush: the happiness of the boy's birth; his velvety smooth cheeks; the shame of having fled him and of having lifted him before dropping him back down again; then his fragile body in the bath; the cushions in the courtyard; her little brother's breath. For the first time, she thought of him as that, *my little brother.* Her grandmother would have been happy to hear her calling him this. She was breathless with emotion. She heard the cooing of the river below and, for the first time, this burbling didn't highlight nature's indifference but rather the permission it was granting her. It was saying:

you can be released from this. So she broke apart. An astonished silence fell upon those gathered. Even the undertakers stopped what they were doing. The firstborn was the first to rush to her aid, stunned by her suffering. Hadn't she decided not to feel anything anymore?

We watch the firstborn race towards the sister, catch her by the shoulders and repeat her name as he tries and fails to get her to stand. He keeps her head buried in his chest. We see nothing but her shaking shoulders as she manages to say: "It took his death to bring us together again." Her elder brother places his hand on her brow and his chin on her head. He smiles despite the tears and says: "No – even dead, he binds us together."

3

The Last-born

THE PARENTS RANG TO TELL EVERYONE: "WE'RE expecting another child." Their voices were full of fear. They chose their words carefully. Not that they should have worried. The firstborn was off living in the city, doing an economics degree, while the sister was away studying in Lisbon.

Since both were absent from home, neither had come across their mother in the middle of the night, curled up on the sofa, clutching her belly. They didn't know that she dreamed of the birth going disastrously wrong. They hadn't seen her march up the mountainside, glassy-eyed, the silence of the evening enveloping her in its wool, her feet cautiously apart so as not to slip. They had no idea that their mother clasped their father's hand when they met the consultant who'd overseen the boy's birth – back in the same hospital, with the same grey rubber floor, and the same question as years before: is everything normal?

The weight of dread hung over these wounded parents, united in a mutual fear that they'd again wreck life while seeking to generate it.

Pointing to the ultrasounds as proof, the consultant told them that nothing seemed wrong. In fact, "It's alright," is what he said. No-one had uttered such a phrase to the parents in years. They thought they must have misheard. They didn't dare to think they'd understood correctly, and asked the consultant to repeat himself. He smiled. What had happened to them had certainly been bad luck. Yet the mother had got pregnant again, despite being aged over forty, which was proof there was good fortune, too. Tragedy, then joy. There was some kind of balance to it after all, the consultant said as he accompanied them to the exit. He appeared genuinely moved. He mentioned the specific examinations the mother would have to undergo. The pregnancy would be very closely monitored. Medical imagery had evolved considerably in ten years and any malformation would show up. Then the consultant cleared his throat and told the parents that he'd hidden a fact from them – "Having such an unusual child is a life-altering ordeal. Most couples don't survive."

And now the new child was there.

It was another boy.

The last-born.

He'd arrived in the wake of tragedy. Therefore, he had no right to cause a fuss.

His behaviour was exemplary. He barely cried. He adapted to inconveniences of all kinds, to being separated from others, even to storms. He never complained about having to work. He consoled his parents. He was the perfect son. He made up for the one who'd gone before him.

His growth and development were a source of tension throughout his childhood. Sometimes, his mother would ask if he could see an orange in the fruit bowl from the other side of the kitchen. And he'd say: "Of course I can." His mother's smile seemed so rooted in the past, dragged down by such sorrow, that he'd carry on describing the orange to keep her happy, so much so that she ended up laughing: "It looks soft," he'd say, "darkish in colour, not completely round, balanced on top of the apples. It might fall, but it's holding on for now."

He grew up hearing sighs of relief. The walls of the house were plastered with photographs of his first steps and the faces he pulled as he uttered new words, of the novel gestures he made. All of this collected as evidence, designed to reassure and calm. He was healthy. The proof was there for all to see: he could walk, speak and see. It was documented.

*

The last-born knew he didn't walk alone. He'd been born in the shadow of a dead child and that shadow cast a ring around his life. He had to put up with it. He didn't begrudge this duality. He absorbed it. A disabled boy had been born before him and survived until the age of ten. The absent were part of his family.

The last-born often got out of bed in the middle of the night, driven by some sort of timeless instinct – no-one slept properly in their family where sleeplessness bore the stamp of heartbreak. His intuition was often right. He'd find his father reading in front of the now cold wood-burner, or discover his mother on the sofa, a blank look on her face, staring at nothing, eyes sweeping emptily over objects. So, he'd sit down beside them to talk gently, or not talk at all. He'd offer to make them a mulberry tea, speak about school, or natter about the accident involving the co-operative truck. The last-born cared for them the way a parent might kneel down beside a sick child's bed. He knew that in an ideal world this shouldn't have been his role, but fate liked to play havoc with roles. It was up to him to adapt. He tried not to think things over too much; he felt no resentment. It was just how life was. There was an inherent goodness to him. The way he appeared to smile at us stones in the sunlight could have led some to believe it was just a form of innocence – but precisely because he looked upon us, and smiled at us, we knew it was nobility: a kindness built on bravery, on a willingness to open up to others. There was a certainty to him, an understanding that the negative judgements of others would not get in his way. Indeed, the strength of his kindness had granted him an independence of spirit. It made him immune to stupidity. He could be sure of his instincts. He had accepted the strange family into which he'd been born. They were wounded but brave people, and he loved them. He would take care of them – his parents, above all.

The bond between the last-born and his parents was strong. They formed a cocoon. They wove their days together into a healing scar. The burden of renewal, heavy and rewarding at the same time, had fallen on the last-born. It was the role he'd been given.

Sometimes, his father would ruffle his hair with a fretful tenderness. The gesture betrayed a fear that the last-born might leave, that he needed to be held back in some way – because before him there'd been suffering, and after him there'd be nothing. The child existed in this in-betweenness: he was both a new start and a continuum, a break and a promise.

His hair wasn't as thick as the dead boy's, nor were his eyes as black, nor his eyelashes as long. He always felt he was "less" than his brother, even though he wasn't the one who'd been born diminished. The last-born carried these thoughts in his mind without any bitterness. He only felt goodwill towards his dead brother and an eagerness to understand more about him. He'd have given a lot to have known him. There was something else, too. He knew that the moments he shared with his parents belonged to him and him alone. They'd emerged with him. They were unsullied, free of memory's shackles, clean of all trace of the ghost. He had no reason to feel robbed of anything.

His father would take him out onto the porch to cut wood. The sound of the chainsaw seemed to clip the air. He loved how the blade grazed the bark before slicing into the wood like butter. The chunks fell with a dull thud. The last-born would lean down and drag the new log towards him while his father grabbed the next trunk to place it on the iron trestles with their jaw-like crosses studded with triangles. Then the boy pushed the wheelbarrow towards the woodshed, opened the worm-eaten door and unloaded the logs, dreamily observing the labels showing the years the wood had been cut: 1990, 1991, 1992 – many years when he hadn't existed.

Often he and his father put on woollen hats and gloves and went out to repair things. This was their great obsession: shoring up, improving, putting stuff right.

They built a drystone wall, as well as steps down to the river, hung a door, fixed handrails and gutters, paved a small terrace. Together they wandered down the aisles of vast DIY shops. Whenever they walked past an advert showing a building in a meadow with a tiled roof and a large gate (the advert was extolling the virtues of perfect roofing), the last-born noticed his father tense. He told himself that a house in a meadow must have played a part in their past. The last-born sensed the same tensing of bodies around him when his mother prepared a fruit compote. Once, in the hardware store car park when a woman unfolded her child's buggy, the catch unfastened so quickly that the rubber wheels slammed into the ground. The father jumped as if the sound had sprung at him from a lost dimension in time, his eyes sweeping the car park in search of the unfolded buggy and the child about to be placed in it. Then he pulled himself together, lowered his head and went through the turnstiles into the hardware store.

The last-born hadn't missed an instant of the scene even though it had all been over in seconds. He'd seen enough to guess.

On the way home, the rear of the car packed with newly bought tools, the last-born and his father sat in satisfied silence, dreaming of future projects and building jobs.

Sometimes, out of the blue, as the road turned towards the village, his father would ask:

"What tool do you use for hand tapping?"

"A wrench."

"How many turns are required?"

"Three."

"What types of hand taps are there?"

"A taper, plug and bottoming tap."

"What does a bottoming tap look like?"

"It has no line on its square end."

And that was it. The father carried on driving while the last-born stared out of the window.

They planted bamboo on the sunniest terrace as a way of preserving the grandmother's memory, though the last-born had never met her. Whenever they worked together, their movements were synchronised, fluid and precise. They handed each other stones or tools in a wordless dance. Sweat ran into the father's eyes and he wiped his forehead without removing his coarse gloves. The sun's rays cracked deep into the earth. That's why the ground shone, the last-born thought. All around them the mountains kept watch. They made their presence known in countless different sounds: whines, creaks and bursts of rage and laughter. They whispered, thundered, purred and crooned. The all-hearing, absent boy must have picked up on these noises. No doubt he'd recognised that every mountain was both witch and medieval princess. As well as gentle ogre and ancient god. And monster, too.

The last-born felt that the mountains around him were his allies. Yet he knew the work of men could easily turn to nothing; that hillside terraces collapsed; that trees grew on rocks and their roots tore up crops. He understood the inexorability of life. He knew, too, that in April the celandines sprinkled their yellow drops in the grass; that the jays pecked at the figs in July; and that in October it was time to crouch down and pick the first chestnuts off the ground. He liked to turn stones over to see what life teemed away beneath them. He'd understood that of us: that we provide shelter. He went as far as to dig holes in the earth, half a foot deep, shielding them with flat stones so that lizards could lay their eggs in safety. He particularly liked millipedes because they rolled up into a ball whenever they got scared. He loved this impulse. It was a source of wonder to him: curling in on yourself when in danger. In fact, he thought, humans imitated millipedes. Whenever he held one in a tiny slate-coloured ball in the hollow of his hand, he barely dared to breathe until he'd placed it back in the damp earth and tiptoed away.

The last-born had immense respect for nature. Stones, to him, carried the weight of creatures past, while the sky provided a limitless sanctuary for birds. The river, meanwhile, was home to toads, grass snakes, pond skaters and crayfish. He never felt alone. He understood that the other boy, too, had lived longer than had been thought possible because he'd experienced nature's abundance. It made sense. Had he been given the chance to know his brother, they'd have had that mutual acceptance of the mountains in common.

Come evening time, the last-born and his parents ate dinner together. He enjoyed the triviality of the words they spoke to one another, the simple fact of being together, the three of them, hearing each other's voices. Their shared tenderness made up for any gaps in the conversation, patched over gentle silences. They poured water for each other, passed the meat and rye bread. They handed round the plate of *pélardon* goat's cheese. Their sentences were punctuated by little outbursts: "Oh really?"; "... The Espérou is very pretty"; "Nettles are so painful, aren't they?"; "... The Mauzargues are a kind lot". They discussed the twin-shaft mixer they'd bought the previous day, wondering whether four hundred and fifty spins per minute was fast enough. When the last-born had opened his sister's desk to look for paperclips he'd come across a notepad with lists of "subjects of conversation". That's exactly what had been written on top of the page. It had surprised him. He and his parents never needed "subjects of conversation" at dinnertime. He drew some secret satisfaction from this – not a pride, more of a comfort. Indeed, he felt there was a seamlessness to his relationship with his parents: the kind of calmness that came with healing.

The sister and the firstborn cropped up a lot in their conversations. It was like they were there without being there. Snippets of news filtered through: communication had become much easier because both siblings had recently acquired mobile phones. The firstborn had a proper job. He wore a jacket and tie, went to work on the bus every day and lived in an apartment on his own. There was no-one else in his life; no love, few friends. The parents talked about this in the way one might handle a delicate crystal vase.

The sister was still in Portugal, though she'd quit her Portuguese literature course. She was fed up with it, the father said. She'd never liked school anyway. She was thinking of giving private French lessons instead. She often went out in the evening. Her apartment looked out onto a steep, narrow street with a vinyl record shop on it. In fact, the owner of that shop had moved in with her. She called less often as a result. She seemed to be in love. "She's reborn," the mother said with a smile. The last-born realised that to be reborn, you had to have thought yourself dead. Once more, he caught a glimpse of the desperate times his family had known before him.

Beneath the faultless exterior he presented to the world, the last-born burned away with countless questions. When did you first notice? What did my dead brother do all day? Did he have a particular smell? Were you sad? How did he eat? Could he see anything? Could he walk a bit? Could he think? Was he in pain? Were you in pain?

In his heart, whenever he thought about his brother, he called him "my almost me". He felt that the dead boy had been his double, someone who resembled him closely; someone who'd only had his senses – indeed his sensitivity – as language; someone who wouldn't have ever hurt a thing, who'd turned inwards. Rather like a millipede.

The strange thing, the last-born realised, was that, despite never having met his brother, he missed him. He'd have given anything to have seen him just once, to have smelled him, touched him – once would have been enough. Then he'd have been on a par with the other members of his family and satisfied his genuine curiosity about the boy. The fact that he'd been born diminished didn't repel him. The last-born valued feebleness and the way weak things were incapable of judging him. Why did he fear judgement, though? He had no idea. Was it because of the shame his siblings, and even his parents, had endured when others, with their overpowering and all-conquering normality, had stared at the boy's push-chair? This shame, he sensed, had been so far-reaching and guilt-inducing ("a shameful shame," he said to himself), that it had been handed down to him through his bloodline. He would have loved to have taken the boy in his arms to protect him. How was it possible to miss someone who'd died before you? The question bewildered him to the point of dizziness.

A photo was stuck on the wall in his parents' room, next to the bed, above his mother's lamp. In it the boy was lying on large cushions in the shade of the courtyard. The picture had been taken from a low angle, at the level of the ground, probably by the firstborn. He noticed the thickness of the large cushion on which his bony knees rested, and that his legs appeared to be spread apart. His arms, too, were wide open, his fists clenched like those of a baby. The boy's small wrists looked like "kindling covered in snow", the last-born thought. There was a softness to his face, with its very pale skin, round cheeks, long black eyelashes and thick dark hair. A hand was flashing by at the bottom of the picture, out of focus. He recognised it as his sister's.

The photo had been taken on a Sunday afternoon with the mountains visible above the wall, their peaks, like bulky necks, craning towards the blueness of the sky. It was a calm scene, but there was something twisted about it at the same time. Was it the legs, and the neck dangling too far back? Or was it fate itself?

When he went to kiss his mother goodnight, the last-born would always glance at the photo, almost fearfully. He'd have liked to let his eyes dwell on it. But he didn't dare. His mother had often invited him to ask questions about the boy, but he had too many of them and didn't know how. In truth, he was worried about upsetting her. He didn't want her memories to trigger another sad smile, like when she'd asked him: "Can you see that orange?" He didn't want to risk asking: "If he hadn't died, would I still have been born?" He hugged his mother and muttered silent promises, solemn pledges of love and support, his eyes shut, nestling in the hollow of her neck.

He excelled at school, though academic work didn't appeal to him much. He found it too organised, too conventional, a little idiotic. Except for history. This was a subject that truly interested him. He could remember dates with ease and get lost in bygone eras; grasp their secrets and subtleties, their ways of thinking. His favourite period was the Middle Ages. And when he found out that people in those days gave actual names to bells and swords, he felt understood as he, too, named the stones around him. That's how children's minds work. They give us identities we never requested. The sound of them – "Costane", "Haute-Claire" and "Joyeuse" – pleases us. To some children, a wall is never just a wall, but a panel of characters.

At primary school, the last-born studied from the Viking era to the end of the Second World War with equal excitement. Any date that marked the beginning of a historical period inspired great feelings of happiness, an impression of travelling through uncharted territory. He knew he was going to learn a new language, as well as different ways of eating and being; of exploring geography; even of understanding the mind. History meant studying the unknown, but it echoed with the realities of his present-day. He felt that he was a mere link in a chain, in an endless line of dancers who'd mapped out the world before him. He loved the idea of being positioned between thousands of lives already lived and thousands more to come. It was comforting to know that he'd no longer be the last to have been born. Sometimes he ran his fingertips over us stones as if he were respectfully touching his ancestors' remains. It was true, to a certain extent, but he didn't speak about this with anyone.

*

A barrier separated him from other children his age. Even so, he didn't find it hard to see through his fellow humans. He was able, at a glance, to spot sadness and longing: feelings of inferiority, secret loves and fear. He sniffed people out like an animal might, but he did his best to stay human, to avoid being rejected. He'd guessed all too well that the hypersensitive were easy prey.

One day, he noticed a lonely boy, the same age as him. No doubt he'd come from another valley or just moved to the area. No-one seemed to know him. The last-born watched as his school peers sized him up, and understood that the new boy, by keeping himself to himself, was in danger. Indeed, in a flash, another boy grabbed his scarf and ran away with it, rolling it into a ball so it could be lobbed from one person to the next. The new boy jumped to grab it with his arms outstretched. The scarf, however, had been tossed up too high. It landed in the last-born's hands. He wanted to help the boy, who was charging towards him, but he did the opposite and copied everyone else. He hurled the scarf as hard as he could towards another group of children, forcing the new boy to make an about-turn so abrupt that he slipped and fell. The boy didn't stand up immediately and lay there crying in humiliation. A wicked joy spread through the playground.

The scene haunted the last-born. That night, he dreamed of it. He woke with a jolt, crept downstairs and settled on the sofa next to his father who, as so often, was up late reading a DIY magazine. The last-born came to hate the incident in the playground and hated himself for it. If he'd been Richard the Lionheart, he thought, he'd never have behaved like that. He could still hear the boy's unforgettable cries as if he were right beside him in the sitting room. It made him feel that he'd lost sight of his true self. The next day he waited for the right moment before entering the classroom, unfurled his scarf and handed it to the new boy in front of the other pupils. He heard someone whisper, "Traitor", and the boy purposefully didn't take the scarf from him. It fell, like a heavy ribbon, onto the corridor floor. The boy didn't become my friend, the last-born thought, and the others stopped liking me, too. Deep down, he wasn't surprised. He was different from other children, and different from the new boy who was also different in his particular way. He had to accept it, and watch his back.

Questions that no-one else seemed to be asking spun round in his head. A stone wall separated the school playground from the road. He stood motionless in front of it wondering how its holes could be patched up. He remembered the words his father used when they built walls together, words that he loved: coping, footing, hearting, through-stone and more. He wanted to get close to the stones and press himself against them, rest his forehead, "Lie down vertically". That's how he described the feeling to himself. Yet he knew he had to hold back, curb his compassion and try and become part of his peer group again. He needed to make up for the scarf incident. So whenever his class kicked a football around, he played along too. He mistrusted others, but he blended into the group to avoid any sort of blame. He nodded when he had to, amused the crowd, and didn't reveal that, while in the cafeteria queue at lunchtimes, he was quietly listing the various routes used by the Crusaders. He exuded just the right amount of cheekiness to offset any resentment about his high grades. His only red line was injustice. His empathy was such that he couldn't bear it. One day, when the class turned on the new boy again, he became angry and warned them that he wouldn't join in. He said that they shouldn't push a loner around. His trembling, cold voice calmed tempers. The last-born even gained some standing as a leader, which he didn't know how to handle. He admitted to no-one that, for a split second, he'd seen the evil such a mob would have inflicted on his maladapted brother.

The last-born invited friends to the hamlet – the new boy, along with others from school. It was the first time children had gathered there in ages. The sister and the firstborn had long stopped inviting anyone over. The mother bought litres of soft drinks; the father cobbled together some stilts. When the new boy fell flat on his face, his legs absurdly stiff and straight, the last-born ignored the general hilarity and felt an overwhelming affection for him instead. The mother seemed to have the same reaction as she helped the boy stand up and dusted his T-shirt down. She was smiling. In fact, her happiness was such that it felt like nothing bad could happen. At that moment, she appeared intoxicated by the noise of the children and busied herself by feeding everyone and introducing new games. When had his parents last watched over children at their house, the last-born wondered? In his mind, the most trivial instances of everyday life could take on a historic or momentous dimension: birthday parties, school fairs, his school reports, even enrolment in archery classes – because to shoot an arrow, you had to stand up straight, see, hold and grasp: all things the dead boy couldn't do. Banal things, when compared to the hardships his family had endured, were a cause for celebration. Yet while they exalted him, placed him on a throne, they crushed him at the same time. He felt like a usurper, and so, all the while, he quietly excused himself to his brother. Sorry to have taken your place. Sorry to have been born normal. Sorry to be alive when you're dead.

*

Some mornings, he stayed in bed and relaxed the back of his neck. Then, slowly, he drew his knees up and stretched them down again, as flat as he could against the mattress. He was mimicking the boy, getting as close as possible to what he must have experienced. He stayed like this, eyes roaming the emptiness, listening out for faint noises like the ruffling of the river or the scratching of a dormouse in the rafters until he heard his mother shout his name.

His brother and sister came for the holidays. The last-born showed them the building jobs he'd undertaken with their father. He summoned them to the woodpile for a demonstration on how to use a bench grinder. He relished seeing them recoil when he turned the speed up.

"There you go," he said, "properly sharpened blades."

"Don't play with that stuff," the firstborn advised him gently.

Although he liked being around his siblings, he was relieved to see them leave after a few weeks. He could then return to his cocoon. But when his siblings were around, he was happy to shed the cocoon and no longer be the centre of attention. He became a peripheral concern; that was understood. He knew to keep quiet during adult conversations. It didn't bother him. It would change again once his brother and sister left. They appreciated more than he did how life could be thrown off balance;

so he was happy to step aside from time to time. He loved to clamber onto his sister's lap – his pretty, spirited and greedy sister. She always brought recipes back from Portugal. She was the queen of orange-scented waffles. She brought much more than waffles, though. She came with a whole world made of smiles, a new language, a different experience of time and the weather, and talk of a yellow and blue city with monasteries and a giant lift. The sister called him "my little enchanter".

She was very affectionate. Unlike their elder brother, who didn't touch anyone, she spent her time kissing him, grabbing him and drawing him to her. She squeezed him tight as if she feared he might disappear.

When they walked in the mountains, she started her sentences with words like: "When I was little". This made his heart tighten. He'd have loved to have known her as a young girl. He'd have enjoyed being around back then instead of the boy, to have been the only younger brother she should have had. His family's past was full of gaps. But that's exactly why he liked studying history because his own story eluded him. He again caught sight of the high ridges his family had scaled without him, those moments he'd never experience, and he saw their suffering – endless sorrows of which he had no inkling, which still haunted those around him.

Before him there'd only been elders. Both the living and the dead were elders. He, meanwhile, was at the end of the chain.

He was able to ask his sister questions about their brother: when did you realise? What did he do all day? Did he have a particular smell? Were you sad? How did he eat? Could he see? Could he walk at all? Could he think? Was he in pain? Were you in pain?

They were walking up on a mountain *draille* in single file, unable to see each other's faces. She'd charged ahead, almost in a fury, as if she were stamping on the ground. He felt the anger in her, but he felt her power, too. She'd learned Portuguese so fast, and now she had friends, went out, listened to music and knew all the bars. She was embracing life and its speed. She liked to sit and sip coffee in cafés and watch the world go by, studying people's expressions, their to-ing and fro-ing. The crowd was as indifferent, dominant and absolute as the mountains around them. A person could suffer atrocious pain; the crowd and the mountains paid no heed. For many years the sister had been angry at this indifference. Now it calmed her. She saw it as non-judgemental acceptance. The basic laws of life were unforgiving, she told him, but they don't condemn you either.

He loved the roundness of her words whenever she slipped into Portuguese, the semi-muffled sound of it.

Some languages were songlike, he thought, and others were harsh. Portuguese, however, seemed to be directed inwards, as if the mouth swallowed the voice back into the throat before the words were uttered, returning them to the speaker's heart instead. In fact, rather like shy people who are happily absorbed in themselves, Portuguese seemed to prefer staying in the warmth of the body rather than expressing itself out in the open. No single sound emerged fully complete. It was a language which pulled back in order to take better control. It was perfectly suited to his sister, the last-born thought.

She answered his questions, describing how the boy's head would rest on the flat stones by the river, and how their elder brother sat reading beside him. Then she told him about the care home in the meadow run by nuns, and the boy's crooked feet, the shallow roof of his mouth, the velvet softness of his cheeks – along with the chalazions, the convulsions, the Depakene, the Rivotril, the Rifamycin, the nappies, the puréed food, the purple cotton pyjamas, the smiles, the pure, contented whimper that emerged from his mouth. She told him, too, about the excruciating stares others shot the boy, all those instances that had passed by without him. The last-born's history was taking shape. He was understanding where he came from. His sister then spoke to him about their grandmother and her thin kimono, her time in Carrapateira, the yo-yo, trees bent double, her big-heartedness. The sister liked to scold him, too, for dawdling, as he was always overturning stones, searching for millipedes in the soil.

They had their walks: Figayrolles, La Jons, the Varans and Perchevent passes, and Malmort where they rounded up the sheep. The sister tracked down the muddy puddles the wild boar used for wallowing. From where the animals had dug she could determine the wind's direction. If the animals settled on the Mediterranean flank of a mountain it was to protect themselves from the freezing northern wind. Through his sister, the last-born felt he was hearing his grandmother speak, discovering her knowledge of the wind.

They jumped over streams; beat their way through white heather; slipped on loose stones. From time to time, a bramble pricked their skin. They knew how to steady their feet and calm their breath. When they reached the plateau, with the sky opening its arms to them and the mountaintops stretching into the distance, the last-born felt lighter and free of questions. That was it, he thought. Everything was as simple as the landscape in front of him, as crystal clear: he was here while the dead boy was not. This awareness came to him without drama or sadness. Theirs was a form of companionship: I'm here while you're elsewhere. It was enough of a bond.

They often settled down to eat in the shade of a shepherd's hut or watched horses wander freely nearby. These were magic moments. The memory of them would mingle with the sound of bells, bleating, neighing and pounding hooves. And not just animal noises. Smells, too, of broom, damp earth and straw as he, the last-born, couldn't help but match his feelings to his senses. He liked to imagine that centuries before there'd been the same sounds, the same light and the same aromas. Some things never changed. Pilgrims from the Middle Ages would have lived through a similar autumn day with its rush of liquid golds. The poplar trees, tapering into yellow, stood like torches on the slopes while bushes burst into thousands of red dots. The mountains had cloaked themselves in orange, speckled with green, revealing to the last-born how October could display its dazzling colours in one fell swoop. A smell of cream and warmth enveloped him. With it came the babbling of a baby and an image of the new boy from school, happy because he'd finally learned to walk on stilts. The last-born closed his eyes for an instant. Then he got up, satisfied, and waved to his sister. The two of them set off again. He watched her thin shoulders rise in rhythm with her steps and breathing, the weight of her heavy dark hair bouncing off her back.

*

On the way home, they passed a cedar tree planted in a rock. The tree swept upwards, slender and lonely. The sister stopped to look at it.

"That one wants to live," she said, turning her face so he saw it catch the copper-coloured light. "Like you."

His sister was quick, funny, brimming with plans for the future. He felt she was embracing life because she'd missed out on it. Since she'd fallen in love, though, she'd taken to interspersing her conversations with long silences. Often the last-born was left with nothing but the sound of her determined, regular footsteps and the rising of her chest until her voice returned and she spoke of the young man she'd met in a music shop, who'd waited for her, understood her, *mended* her. You can love a person without fearing a disaster will befall them, she said. You can give without fearing loss. You can't permanently live with your fists clenched, waiting for danger. That's what this love has taught me, she said, and what our elder brother doesn't want to understand. Our elder brother, she muttered, who's given up.

The last-born came back from these walks a little dazed. His sister's words would carry on seeping into him over the course of the day. He let them have the time they needed. At supper, he now looked at his elder brother in a different light. His gentle manner and composure had taken on new meaning. How could he have cared so much for the boy when he ignored his actual living brother? One evening, as their father was doling out soup, he asked his elder brother why he no longer read books. The firstborn smiled gloomily – in truth, gloomy smiles were all he ever gave. But the last-born felt entitled to more. So he dared to say: "Books open you up. They free you. If you're no longer reading them it's because you're completely locked inside yourself." The father held the ladle mid-air in astonishment. The sister and mother glanced at one another. The elder brother didn't express any surprise. He nudged his fork to one side by a millimetre or so, then raised his dark eyes and said in a harsh voice:

"We once had a little boy here who really was locked inside himself. He taught us a lot. So don't try and teach me any lessons."

The last-born stared down at his plate. He could feel the dead boy's ghost hovering above the table. He'd never have thought a ghost could hold such power. He addressed his dead brother, inside his head: "What power you had for a maladapted child … you're the one who's the enchanter."

He spoke to his dead brother from a place deep within him. Intuitively, he used tender, simple words, cradled the boy, spoke to him as if he were a baby – although he did also tell him about Richard the Lionheart's death and the code of chivalry used by knights as both those came naturally to him. From afar, no-one would have guessed the last-born was speaking to the boy. He'd describe his visions, match colours to sounds, and tell him what he was feeling. He disclosed his inner world in the full belief he was being understood. You can only share exceptional knowledge with exceptional beings, he told himself. He'd have given anything to touch him. His sister had described the chalky plumpness of his skin, how their elder brother would lay his cheek against his. He imagined the boy's translucent torso, the blue-veined transparency of his wrists, the slenderness of his ankles, the pinkness of the soles of those feet that had never walked on ground. Sometimes he went into the boy's room, which had been converted into an office. His parents had kept the little bed with the white iron swirls. He placed one hand on the mattress, exactly where the boy's head would have been, and closed his eyes. The thread of a crystal-clear singing voice pierced the air and he could hear a smile. A smell of sweat from between the folds of a neck came to him, followed by orange blossom and boiled vegetables. Yet he knew that the moment he lifted his hand to touch his brother's skin and feel his thick hair, the boy would vanish. It was enough to bring tears to his eyes.

One day he asked his mother where the purple cotton pyjamas had gone. Astounded that he had any knowledge of these things, she told him his elder brother had taken them away.

As time went by, the last-born's senses overwhelmed him more and more. The colours of the mountain seeded extravagant poems in him. Glaring sunlight turned to cries so loud that in summer, by eight in the evening, he had to cover his ears. Shade could envelop him in cello music, while smells, all those inescapable fragrances, reawakened long-vanished songs. He wondered whether his brother's nostrils had been filled with similar scents. It was likely, as his sense of smell was fully developed. He'd never know for sure. He found he had an irrepressible urge to describe what he saw around him to his brother. It was as if a power had been bestowed upon him. He had to relay what he saw, out of solidarity and love. The firstborn had reacted in the same way, his sister had said. He, too, described everything to the boy.

The sight of purple, white and yellow flowers thrust him into a world of pistils and fragrances where smells became touch, where forgotten places pulsed with life, in a heady, intoxicating mix – and the spell would only be broken when he heard his mother's voice calling him. When he wanted to explain to her the feelings the world provoked in him, he could only manage to list the flowers' names in their garden. No other words accompanied the riot of purples, bright yellows and creamy whites. His words simply dissolved into phonetic dullness: Althea, Forsythia and Lagerstroemia.

"What a phenomenal memory you have," his mother said. "You remember everything."

"No," he replied, "I just don't forget anything – that's different."

He was clearly advanced for his age. "How can I be ahead when I'm the last-born? That's absurd," he told the psychologist. As with his sister, the parents had noticed a difference between him and his peers and sought professional help. But the psychologist took the comment as a sign of pretentiousness. The boy wanted to tell the therapist that part of him wasn't nine years old, but a thousand years old, and that another part of him was only just waking up; and the gap between these sides of himself, the balancing act he had to perform, cut him off from those around him. He felt different. He envied his classmates who were unmoved by beauty or pity. Why did none of them react to a bird of prey in the sky, to portrayals of gallant kings or the dinner lady's smile in the cafeteria? Was it possible that the world's turmoil made no noise in their head, that it struck no chord?

Even the new boy at school now played with those who'd stolen his scarf. No one seemed bothered that they were alone. Being an enchanter certainly cut you off from others.

He waited until the Easter holidays to discuss it with his sister. But she didn't come. She'd gone travelling with her new boyfriend. He missed the sensation of her hand on the back of his neck. He turned to the firstborn instead. Maybe it was for the best anyway, as he needed someone as profoundly damaged as his elder brother to understand what he was going through. But the first-born wandered off saying that he was going on a walk on his own.

He followed him. The firstborn never went far, only to the riverbank, to the spot where the stones were flat. He sat down, hugged his knees to his chest and didn't budge. The last-born hung around in the shadows to observe him. Again he felt jealous of the dead boy. If I'd been disabled, he thought, my brother would have looked after me. Then he bowed his head; he was ashamed for having such thoughts.

The sister rang one evening towards the end of the summer. The mother looked pale when she hung up. She sat back down at the table and cleared her throat. "Your sister is pregnant," she said. "The tests are fine. All is well." The father stood and embraced his wife. The last-born felt as if he'd been struck down. He imagined his sister would stop loving him – that the future baby would take his place. Another era of renewal had begun. The new birth would rob him of his position in the family. He would no longer serve any purpose. He stood up, grabbed an orange from the fruit bowl, opened the door and hurled it as hard as he could into the courtyard, at us.

It was the first and only act of rebellion of his life. When he turned back towards the kitchen and saw his parents' anxious and tense faces, he swore he'd never do such a thing again.

When Christmas comes round again, the siblings slip out through the glass doors into the courtyard and leave the overheated racket of the house behind. The old uncles have died. The cousins now have children of their own. The tradition of playing music, of Protestant chants and feasts, has carried on.

The siblings stand with their backs to us, shivering in the cold, while one of the cousins adjusts the camera lens. The sister laughs while rubbing her elder brother's shoulders and placing her other hand on the back of the last-born's neck.

She then cradles her pregnant belly, her head tilted to

one side. Her lips are pink, her forehead held high. She has a hint of a smile. She's wearing a grey polo neck, her hair over her shoulders.

The firstborn is standing straight with his arms crossed. His face remains inscrutable apart from the kindly eyes behind his thin tortoiseshell glasses. He has narrow shoulders, short dark hair, and is wearing the sort of shirt you'd expect from a head of finance.

The last-born is sticking his chest out, as if he's marching towards the camera. His face is round with a big mischievous smile. His eyes are a little intense, his lips stretched across metal braces. His lighter, scraggly hair is blowing in all directions.

All three siblings have dark circles around their big, slightly almond-shaped eyes, their irises so dark they have merged with their pupils.

Everyone got a printed copy of the photo. When the last-born received his, he thought that there had always been the same number of children in their family photos. It was just that the third child had changed.

Later, after she'd given birth to a baby girl, the sister and the last-born put their walking boots on again and headed off into the mountains. They rediscovered the coolness of mornings, the folding and refolding of discoloured maps, eyes set on ridges and passes above them. While his sister walked ahead on the path, the last-born asked her whether she'd feared giving birth to a child with disabilities. "Strangely not," she said, "mostly because Sandro and I were pretty clear: if there'd been a problem with the baby, we weren't going to keep it. Also I'd lived through that already. The fear had gone. I had the right instincts and a sort of survival guide to it. Fear comes from the unknown." Her words flowed quickly; she felt no need to decorate them with added images or sounds. It was so straightforward. He was able to ask her about being a mother, her new country, her new love. Everything was new with her. Yet newness didn't provoke fear in her. How, he wondered, had she learned to get over the anxiety of looking after a newborn? "We had a baby for ten years, didn't we?" she said. "Even if I didn't get that involved. Anyway, it's the effort you put into raising kids that counts. The end result may be imperfect, or not, that's not important. What counts is how much you invest in it. Sandro's parents separated when he was a kid. His father was poor. He only ever lived in one room. But he remembers how his dad found a folding screen somewhere to make a bed with foam and crates. He turned a corner of his only room into a place for his son. That's got to be better than an absent father who leaves a tin of caviar in the fridge for his kid, isn't it? I feel ready to try as hard as I can for my child, just as our parents did. It doesn't really matter if I succeed or not. That's not the point. It's how much I'm prepared to put into it, to forge a friendship, a love, a new bond." And while she was on the subject of bonds, the sister made it clear she had no intention of getting married to Sandro, "Because just being together, as a couple, despite what some would have us believe, already gives us the greatest freedom. It's the only area of life that's not subject to the usual norms, unlike work and society. You'll find couples who argue endlessly but stay together. Others who thrive in silence. Others still who want children and those who don't. Some who think being faithful is paramount while others don't care at all. What some find banal, others believe to be abnormal. And vice versa. There are as many standards as there are couples. Why try and squeeze this freedom into some kind of official framework?" She spoke like this, in long outbursts of indignant rage, without listening. How did life thump away inside her like this, the last-born asked himself. What miraculous routes had her spirit taken all these years, to be able to blaze as vigorously as the day it was born?

He loved listening to his sister. He thought that she, like their elder brother, and indeed himself, carried a thousand years of life inside her. He began laughing all on his own, thinking about their odd family. He told his sister and she laughed, too, or so it seemed, as he could only see her back on the path ahead of him. People here walked alone. They were no different than the mountain paths they took.

The months slipped by the way they do for a child growing up in the mountains. In January he fell into the river. Then he discovered a litter of kittens for the first time hidden inside the mill. He recognised the start of the wild boar hunt by the blast of a single-shot Baikal rifle. He kept an eye out for foxes, bats and badgers. He marvelled at how autumn stripped the poplar trees, casting their sheath of leaves off in a night. He felt the warm June rain fall in a velvet curtain. He patched up the drystone walls he'd built with his father the previous season. In September he danced around towering bonfires of dead branches along the river, listening to how they whistled like musical instruments when the air was sucked out of them.

But some things didn't change.

The last-born felt escorted at all times. It wasn't just that the mountains bewitched him more and more, but that whatever he felt, touched or smelled, he thought of the boy. Every so often, he'd shut his eyes to focus on the sounds around him. Little enchanter, he thought, I never knew I had to close my eyes to see better. His dead brother was now his invisible companion. He had settled into his life. That was just how it was: some absences were like motherlands and the last-born was returning home.

He found it harder and harder to hide how different he was from those around him. Did others know, for instance, that the mountains had witnessed history from the beginning of time, that this was intrinsic to them – and that his understanding of such things was so anchored in him that he knew the dead never fully disappeared? How could he tell others that the life that teemed away in the mountains had remained unchanged for centuries; that every tiny movement of any animal held the memory of death? Perhaps it was too much to expect of people. Yet, like wild animals, they had a gift for sniffing out his difference. One day his biology teacher asked the pupils to bring a fish into school to dissect. The last-born appeared holding a plastic bag with a trout wriggling away inside. They looked at him in astonishment: everyone else had gone to the fishmonger. No-one had realised that the last-born only knew of fish that swam freely in rivers.

He made words up. A shepherd became a "sheepist"; he described himself as a "dreamist"; he said the colour "bluink" existed (pink with bluish tints); that there was a missing tense called the "future interior". He entrusted

his discoveries to the boy, in whispers, in his old bedroom, with one hand flat against the mattress where his
head would have rested. He went through words and each
sound became a butterfly, a moth, a lacewing, a tiny insect
that fluttered in and out of the white swirls of the bed.
He thanked his brother for this miracle.

As he finished school tests before anyone else, remembered every detail and understood everything he'd been
taught, he had time in class to invent more words and
write them down in secret. His marks were so outstand-
ing none of his peers bothered resenting him. He couldn't
have cared less about competing with them and he
willingly gave his homework out for others to copy. Then
there was his sense of humour. That was his best shield.
He mimicked, fooled around, made fun of situations, and
was so good at self-deprecation that any ill-intentioned
pupils gave up attacking him and burst out laughing
instead. He carried on being invited to other people's
houses and didn't miss a single party, but for a time he
refrained from bringing classmates back to the hamlet.
It struck him as indecent. Outsiders wouldn't have fitted
into the enchanter's kingdom. His awareness of his
difference drew him closer and closer to the boy. He
marvelled at the unlikely bond between them. He wasn't
mad, he knew, but he had to admit that whenever he

spoke to the dead boy it was the only time he felt he wasn't pretending. It was the same with animals. He didn't panic when a bat skimmed his hair or when he accidentally stepped on a toad that had wandered onto the road. He stood stock still while his sister's children let out wild screams, the toad's glistening eyes swivelling. The last-born knew the shouts bothered the creature and he carried it to the river, his screeching nieces in tow.

He was genuinely happy for the birds when dawn turned into a beautiful day. Standing at the water's edge, he'd close his eyes and listen to their chirping. In those moments, his sister forbade her children from disturbing him. She didn't say, "he's resting" or "he's being quiet", but rather, "he's breathing".

The last-born loved watching his sister become a mother. He observed her soothing, all-enveloping gestures and understood more about how they'd cared for the boy. So that was the smell deep inside the folds of a baby's neck; those were the clenched fists; and those the tiny sounds of a newborn mammal sucking, hiccuping, moaning and breathing fitfully. He particularly liked babies' arms, their loose wrists, how they moved like Balinese dancers, slow and taut at the same time. He thought that all warriors since time began had once been small beings capable of twirling like dancers. He imagined the anguish his family must have felt before his nieces said their first words or stumbled taking their first hesitant steps. What pain it must have caused to be in the permanent state of a newborn, as if time were denying itself. And all the while his brother's body had continued to grow, as if to add a layer of mockery to his impaired state.

Yet what his sister had told him about her role as a mother seemed true – she wasn't worried. The fevers, the coughs, the wheezing, the skin rashes and stomach aches: these were part of an adventure she handled with calm and resolve. Even level-headed Sandro relied on her. Was it because her children were girls and their gender set them further apart from the loss of her brother? Did this make her mothering easier? Perhaps. The fact was his sister knew what she was doing. The gestures, the expressions and the lullabies came naturally to her. The last-born sometimes felt his sister lacked imagination with her children. He would have liked to have seen her give in to chaos a bit more rather than be a tireless and fearless soldier. But then he remembered how he'd once found her notebook and left it at that. He admired her. He could only think that, having seen it all, she no longer feared anything.

He no longer feared much either. His place in the family was secure. His sister had had the astuteness not to take anything from him in order to give it to her children. The two of them still had their walks in the mountains and their conversations. The last-born was considerate enough not to request more than that; to give her the freedom to be the kind of parent she wanted to be. One thing continued to intrigue him, however: why did she so often hold her children by the back of the neck instead of guiding them by the hand? Why did she touch their necks even when she was giving them a cuddle? She took a few steps forward before replying, as they were out on a mountain *draille*, but her voice was loud enough for him to hear from behind.

"Because one day I wanted to carry him and I grabbed him under the arms and his neck jerked back. His head was left dangling. I got scared, let go, and the rear of his skull smacked against the fabric of the rocker chair. My memory of his limp neck swinging freely is so dreadful, the way it hung loose, his head dragged forward, hunching his body over, folding in on itself. I hadn't been able to hold his neck. I hadn't understood how weak that part of his body was – only joined to the rest of his body like the string of a marionette. What if his neck had snapped? Can you imagine? So that's why."

When his sister's daughters were around, the house filled with joyful shouts, the sound of Portuguese and a smell of waffles. The parents eagerly awaited each holiday as a result. The last-born then fashioned swords, drafted cards on Richard the Lionheart and prepared a heraldry competition. Even the firstborn, who was so sensitive to noise, joined in the games. He was the one who checked that the children's bicycle brakes worked; that the swing seat was secure; that the banks of the river weren't too slippery. He was particularly attentive to the needs of his sister's second child who seemed as quiet and wordless as he was. She enjoyed brain teasers and puzzle-solving and he'd patiently help her, choosing his words with care, bending down to tie up her laces.

One day, the last-born discovered this niece and the firstborn sitting together in the shade of the courtyard. The two of them were poring over a sudoku book. The firstborn was speaking softly, a frown of concentration on his face, a pencil pointed at the open page. The little girl, dark brown hair over her shoulders, was resting her head against the firstborn's forearm and staring intently at the squares filled with numbers. They were so focused on the page that the last-born hardly dared breathe. In the stillness of the summer air, only the river made a whirring sound on the other side of the wall. That's when the last-born spotted his sister at the other end of the courtyard, standing in the medieval doorway. She, too, was studying the firstborn with her daughter, both of them unaware they were being observed from both sides.

His sister was just *checking*, the way a general might inspect the troops. She saw the last-born. Without taking his eyes off her, or moving towards her, he raised his thumb in a sign of victory. She'd achieved the renewal she wanted.

During the summer months, they placed the two thick cushions they'd used for the boy in the courtyard. The nieces snuggled up together on them or jumped from one cushion to the other. The third girl – the youngest – took her naps on them. We sometimes saw a look of sorrow spread across the firstborn's and the sister's faces. Of course, they were seeing another body, which appeared to be asleep but was not, knees apart, high arches on the feet, hair ruffled by the breeze. But on the cushion was an ordinary girl of two years old, who was rubbing her eyes and asking for a snack.

When the young family set off for Lisbon again, and his elder brother went back to the city, the last-born resumed his former ways. Once again he and his parents ate supper alone, the three of them together, undisturbed by anyone else. He settled back into the steady flow of small daily pleasures, relishing the prospect of long evenings when he'd have time to study history or learn the language of heraldry. As if making up for lost time, he revived his kinship with the boy, deep within himself.

He set about describing the associations he noticed in nature, the hidden folds of the mountains, the wild boar by the ponds, the millipedes under the stones. He was back in familiar territory, and that territory was his dead brother. Essentially, there were four of them in the house: his parents, him and the boy. Who could have said otherwise?

One evening, during the Easter holidays, a storm broke over the mountains. The thunder beat its drums across the dark sky flecked with lightning. So much rain fell, and so suddenly, that the river swelled. Water the colour of chocolate surged forth. Its current ripped the bark from the lower parts of the trees lining the banks, leaving them bare. The water's stampede carried branches and pebbles as it scraped the terrace on the grandmother's old house. We, the stones, held firm. We knew one of us was going to be dislodged from the wall and left to roll onto the slate stones below, to be rocked back and forth. The wind was our real enemy, though. It always had been. It was even more powerful than fire or water, both of which we feared less. The wind can truly pick stones apart.

The flashing lights of fire engines pierced through the rainy fog. An electric pylon had tipped onto a roof in a remote hamlet. A car had been swept away by the flooding and was blocking all access. It rained so hard that narrow waterfalls, as taut as cutting wire, streamed down the slopes onto the roads. The fire engine, its roof pummelled by rain, had nearly rammed into the bridge.

Everyone was familiar with nature's outbursts of rage. That afternoon, the father had parked the cars further up the hill, placed his power tools on high shelves, boarded up the woodshed, brought the garden furniture in and opened all the cellar windows – as water always had to flow; it couldn't be confined. The family, minus the sister, stood by the windows looking out on the river, trying to gauge how much it would rise; ready to act if it reached dangerous levels. They didn't take their eyes off the water. The last-born had taken refuge in the boy's bedroom. He watched the trees twist in the wind. The pines were flapping their branches up and down like birds about to take off. He let himself be filled with the roar, desperately hoping all the while that the wild animals had managed to find shelter. He remembered the places he'd seen nests and hideaways, the pools beside the river where the toads spawned, the fox dens, the wild boars' wallowing holes, and the crevices in the walls where the lizards hid. What would be left? The water had battered everything, depriving his fellow creatures of safety. The millipedes would surely have curled up in balls only to be spun and rolled away by the rain.

He jumped. There was a loud knocking on the court-yard door.

A shepherd appeared, wearing a long waterproof coat and a wide-rimmed leather hat dripping with rainwater. He shook the father's hand. He explained in a loud voice, drowned out by thunder, that he'd been looking for one of his ewes for several days. Now he'd discovered it in the old mill. It had taken cover from the storm. The animal was ill. Could someone help him lift it onto his truck? Of course, the father said, I'll fetch the boys.

The two sons put on boots and tugged their hoods down. Outside the great downpour continued, interlaced with rumbling. They walked with their heads bowed. The rain hammered their shoulders like a furious toddler's fists. Sheets of hurrying water coiled round their ankles. They pressed on and crossed the bridge. Beneath them, the river ripped along in brown bubbles. They took the left terrace to the mill, ducking to get through the low door.

The last-born felt as if he were entering a cold cave filled with silence and shade. Water was running down the stones around them. Only the rain's rattling could be heard. He sensed a presence in the darkness. The ewe was there, lying flat, its brown flank abnormally large, while its legs seemed thin and its hooves glossy. The animal was panting, which swelled its belly even further. He couldn't help but touch it. The wool was soft. The ears, pierced by a plastic tag, felt velvety. The ewe had its eyes closed. The last-born gently ran his finger over one of its rounded eyelids, brushing the long, black lashes. Its lower lip quivered. Its short breaths matched the drumming of the rain. The sounds were one and the same to him, like a gentle trotting. Perhaps it was life scampering away, he thought. He saw some hands shaking large, green and shiny tarpaulin sheets in front of him. His father's voice snapped him out of his thoughts and brought him back to the mill: "Help me get her out of here."

They grabbed the hooves, counted to three and lifted the creature up. The ewe was heavy. The shepherd had opened the back doors of his truck. The misty shape of the firstborn's silhouette appeared. He was waiting for them, his hood covering his face.

As they moved away from the mill, the ewe's head slipped off the father's forearm and swung loose. For a second, the full weight of its exhausted, washed-out flesh could be felt, dangling grotesquely in the void, the skin on the neck stretched and tight. They stepped back to gain some momentum and heaved the body upwards. The whole truck shook as they let it go.

"Meteorism," the father said to the shepherd, as he leaned over to get his breath back.

The shepherd nodded.

"Alfalfa or cloverleaf?" the father asked, but as if he were only talking to himself. "It's meteorism either way."

The last-born would normally have relished such a word, but he was no longer listening. He was transfixed by his brother's tall figure inside the truck. He had removed his hood and was leaning over the ewe as it breathed more and more quickly. White foam was spilling from the corner of its mouth. The firstborn lay down beside it, placed his forehead against its face and stroked the bloated belly. His hand looked like a pale stain moving back and forth on a dark fabric. He mumbled to it as the last-born looked on. The firstborn's black hair was blending with the animal's dark wool. It seemed as if the rain was falling more heavily, cutting them off from the world outside. My brother succours the broken, he thought, he's doing what suits him best.

The father, slightly embarrassed, let the conversation with the shepherd linger long enough for the firstborn to clamber to his feet, look back at the ewe and shut the truck doors behind him.

"Let us know how it goes," the father said, and the shepherd tapped the brim of his hat.

The truck drove away. The headlights blurred into the night and vanished. The mother's voice was calling them. They headed back to the house. As they entered the courtyard, with the wind finally dropping and the rain weakening, we, the stones, noticed the last-born reach for his elder brother's hand, and have it held in return.

At dinner, the last-born became bolder still. With his heart thumping, he leaned his head against his brother's shoulder and the firstborn didn't budge. The mother reached for her mobile and took a photo. She sent it to her daughter and whispered happily in the father's ear so no-one else could hear:

"Our life's work: one wounded, one rebellious, one maladapted, and the last one an enchanter."

CLARA DUPONT-MONOD studied ancient French at the Sorbonne, and began her career in journalism writing for *Cosmopolitan* and *Marianne*. Her novels often draw on medieval myths and history, and have been nominated for the Prix Goncourt and the Prix Femina, two of France's most prestigious literary awards. Her first novel to be translated into English, *The Revolt*, which tells the story of Eleanor of Aquitaine, was published in 2020. She lives in Paris.

BEN FACCINI is a novelist, writer and translator. He is the author of several books, notably *The Water-Breather* (Flamingo, 2002) and *The Incomplete Husband* (Porto-bello, 2007), and is the translator of Lydie Salvayre's *Cry, Mother Spain* (MacLehose Press, 2016) and Mahi Binebine's *The King's Fool* (MacLehose Press, 2020).